What are

Tettegouche

"The book kept me on the edge of my seat. I couldn't put it down."   P. M. Rochester, MN

"I loved it. Wonderful descriptions of people and places, interesting story; well done."   J.K. Blaine, MN

"The story moves effortlessly between converging timelines; finished it in one night."   L. B. Superior, WI

"The author does a masterful job of setting the stage for my mental imagery as I read it from cover to cover."   M. W. Detroit Lakes, MN

"A splendid read. I couldn't put it down."
                                                 S. R. Two Harbors, MN

"The author knows the area, researched the history and spun a classic murder mystery; a good story well told."   S. S. St. Paul, MN

Tettegouche

Where only fear survives

A novel by Tom Baumann

ISBN – 9781731324788

Available from Amazon e-books and in paperback; and select
Minnesota State Park Nature Stores

Prelude

It's known as the Arrowhead. Not for the roving bands of Ojibwe that for 500 years eked out a meager existence in a region that produces paralyzing cold in the winter and suffocating clouds of mosquitoes and black flies in the summer, but for its symmetry. It's a triangular wedge of land that comprises one of the most rugged and remote areas in the United States.

Its southern boundary begins at the port city of Duluth and for nearly 150 miles traces the ragged north shore of Superior, the greatest of the great lakes. The apex of the arrowhead is located near Grand Portage, site of the historic trading post that served as jumping off point for the nine mile carry traveled by French voyageurs to enter the pristine wilderness searching for a bounty of animal furs. From there, its northern frontier follows the international border, established by the Treaty of Paris in 1783 as it hop scotches through an impenetrable wilderness abounding in nearly countless lakes and rivers before reaching the mill town of International Falls. From there, the triangle is closed, by an imaginary line that heads to the south and east landing back in the town of Duluth.

Enticed by seemingly inexhaustible natural resources, miners from Eastern Europe followed the French fur trappers to the Arrowhead, eager to exploit rich veins of iron ore. Then came the timber men from Nova Scotia and Maine, and railroad entrepreneurs from England and Scotland. Swedes and Finns, Italians and Irish joined the bands of Native Americans creating a thick ethic stew seeking fortune, adventure or simply survival. For some, the Arrowhead became the parchment upon which their dreams and fortunes were written and retold. For twin brothers, whose physical traits were as identical as their life paths were different, that dream would become a nightmare.

Chapter 1

broad-shouldered white-tailed deer cautiously picked its way through the dense tangle of hazel brush and alder. Its head was crowned with a magnificent set of nearly symmetrical antlers, its neck thick; a harbinger of the approaching rut. As the wary buck threaded its way through the forest, it sniffed the cool fall air as its ears twitched; senses alert for any smell or sound that might foretell danger. Then, from the direction of the setting sun a baleful, heart-wrenching wail floated in on the gentle westerly breeze. The deer froze as the eerie sound grew louder and more disturbing. Then, as quickly as it had come, it stopped. A few seconds later, the sharp crack of snapping branches and other worldly grunts arose from the opposite direction. Near the top of a low, rocky outcrop a strange figure appeared, clawing its way through the thick brush. The deer bounded off.

Beneath his stiff canvas jacket, Martin's heavy wool shirt clung to his skin like tar paper on a sun-baked roof. Warm droplets of sweat trickled down his forehead. Struggling through the thick curtain of trees and brush, he was startled by a sound that seemed completely out of place in this rough and raw wilderness. He froze; confused and a bit frightened. It was then that he spotted movement to his right as the flag of a retreating deer fluttered in the distance. He was certain that a deer could not make such a noise, but then, what did?

Now at pause, he realized how exhausted he had become. He looked for a place to rest. Ahead, a slab of bedrock, smooth and grey broke the surface of the ridge top oddly imitating a humpback whale breaching calm ocean waters. The outcrop, polished smooth by centuries of passing glaciers would provide an oasis, a convenient place to rest, and relieve his throbbing back of the heavy pack he had been lugging for the last four hours.

Dog's hair; that's what settlers called the nearly impenetrable flush of new growth that had sprung up after the logger's axe had felled the stately pine forests of northeastern Minnesota. Sunlight, now unimpeded, bathed the forest floor, encouraging thrifty stands of aspen and birch, hazel and alder to grow thick amongst the sea of enormous stumps that memorialized the monarchs of the forest, now departed.

Deep scratches to his face and hands offered painful evidence of the gauntlet he had endured as he had slowly pushed his way toward Tettegouche Camp as a hazy October sun coursed its way across the sky. Now, from his perch on the whale's back, he could see that more of the same lay ahead. "Damn my brother," he blurted out to the rocks and trees that surrounded him.

Martin was no woodsman. He was a city doctor who spent his days surrounded by buildings and people. Now as he stumbled through mile after mile of demoralizing wilderness he again questioned his motives, and even his sanity. He had come because a brother he'd not seen in 10 years, in whom he shared little, and honestly cared less, had begged him to come. He shook his head in amazement.

Martin and Matts were twins, born with identical physical features. They were tall, well over six feet, lean and blond, with bright sky-blue eyes. Even now, the only physical attribute that defined them was facial hair; Martin maintained a neatly trimmed goatee while Matts, contrary to popular fashion, was always clean shaven.

Growing up, Martin was the quiet one; blessed with a brilliant mind tempered by suffocating caution and a deeply introverted nature. In stark contrast, Matts was simple-minded, gregarious and fearless, to the point of recklessness. As adventurous as Martin was wary, Matts charged through life unafraid; expecting good luck and success would find him, and for some inexplicable reason it did.

From an early age, their father Olaf, expected that one of his sons would become a doctor; a surgeon like his own father had been in Sweden. It was obvious which son that would be, and with unrelenting prodding and cajoling, Martin reluctantly agreed; attending the University of Minnesota's Medical School. Following graduation, he returned to Duluth to take up practice at the well-respected St. Luke's Hospital, located in the heart of the growing downtown area.

Now as Martin rested on the whale's cold hard back, his breathing slowed and his skin began to cool. He dabbed at the droplets of sweat and streaks of blood that clung to his cheeks and forehead as he sized up the forbidding forest that confronted him. For a moment, a sudden urge to retreat and abandon this fool's errand came over him. But for reasons that seemed to defy logic, he decided that he could not give up now, that he must push on.

As he readied himself to dive back into the bush, he dug a magnetic compass from his pocket. Slipping the fine instrument from its leather sleeve, he again appreciated the ornate brass case that protected its delicately balanced needle. It was a needle always in

11

search of true north; but not here, not in this place. For Martin was just another victim of what the native Ojibewe called misaabe, or sleeping giant, a unique feature of northeastern Minnesota that had confounded government land surveyors decades earlier.

Lying undetected beneath thousands of square miles of forest land to the north and west of Tettegouche Camp is an enormous geologic anomaly laid down a billion years ago. It wasn't until prospectors in the 1880s seeking rich veins of gold discovered a different sort of deposit; iron ore, high in mineral content and close to surface. For those using a magnetic compass to navigate the trackless forest, the ore created a mystery that defied explanation. Now as Martin attempted to set his bearings he was thwarted by a compass needle that danced like a drop of water on a hot skillet, providing little help or direction. He would have to depend on the sun and dead reckoning to guide him.

Suddenly the caterwauling of a noisy jay, its royal blue feathers puffed full to ward off the morning chill, snapped Martin from his thoughts. As he struggled to his feet, his back protested vigorously, the muscles in his legs burned. From his crude map, he estimated that at least another grueling mile stood between him and the collection of three small lakes that surrounded Tettegouche Camp. Willing himself to ignore the pain, he called upon a dwindling pool of determination and dove back into the bush.

He had not gone very far, when the thicket behind him erupted in sound that caused Martin to think that a runaway railcar, inexplicably, was plowing its way through the dense forest. Now a deep, throaty bellow and an ominous series of grunts joined in the cacophony. Martin's throat tightened; his heart began to beat wildly. What could it be? He couldn't even guess.

But whatever it was, his impulse was to run; but where? As he looked around, the thick brush that surrounded him formed prison walls, cutting off his escape. Desperate now, as the commotion of snapping branches and deep grunts grew closer, Martin threw himself behind a huge, rotting stump, burrowing his face into the moist, cool ground.

Chapter 2

Flowing from Seven Beaver Lake in the heart of iron country, the St. Louis River rambles through deep shadowy forests, lush green sedge meadows and eruptions of bedrock as it navigates a 192 mile journey to Lake Superior. After a final frantic run through rocky rapids the river collides with Lake Superior's most western point. It was there, that a fur trapper named Daniel Greysolon Sieur du Lhut, known to his comrades as DuLuth, would lend his name to the ramshackle hamlet that in the 1850's began to form on the long open slope overlooking the western finger of Lake Superior.

For the next 40 years, Duluth was the definition of a boomtown; riding an economic rollercoaster that brought hope and despair in equal measure. For a time in the mid 1870's it nearly dried up and blew away. But good fortune struck when railroad access to the west coast was established with the completion of the Transcontinental Railroad and Jay Cooke's Lake Superior and Mississippi Railroad connecting Duluth with St. Paul. Duluth became the only port in the country with water and rail access to both the Atlantic and Pacific Oceans.

Soon the timber and mining industries exploded, and a sprawling web of rail lines ferried a steady stream of immigrant workers into the Arrowhead eager to drain the region of iron ore, timber, fish and furs. Dr. Thomas Preston Foster, founder of the first newspaper in Duluth, coined the expression "The Zenith City of the Unsalted Seas" and by the 1890's, Duluth was the fastest growing city in the country.

At the dawn of the 20th century, the Zenith City was home to ten newspapers, six banks and a dazzling new eleven-story architectural behemoth named the Torrey Building. Almost 60,000 inhabitants called Duluth home, creating a diverse, thriving community with commerce and trade flowing through the city in every direction. Duluth, it was reported, was now home to more millionaires per-capita than any city in the United States.

And so it was in the spring of 1910, a group of these wealthy and ambitious men, during an especially energetic discussion fueled by hubris and expensive bottles of Hennessy cognac, hatched a plan to construct a lodge in the heart of the Minnesota's northeastern wilderness.

The men were gathered, as they did each month, in a well-appointed suite on the 8th floor of the Spalding Hotel. Known simply as The Spalding to the locals, the massive, castle-like hotel was built in a style described as an 'artistic blending of Gothic, Corinthian, and Egyptian styles.' It would soon become a popular address for local businessmen as well as visiting investors and land agents. Many a real estate transaction took place within its thick dark walls.

The group of seven men was known far and wide as the Duluth Venture Club. Drawn together by mutual self-interest they met at the Spalding to gossip, engineer business deals, and retell well-worn stories of previous exploits and accomplishments. It was Arlo Peterson, owner of Comstock-Peterson Logging Co. who

15

broached the idea of a wilderness camp.

Peterson was nearly sixty years old, though he neither looked nor acted such an advanced age. He possessed a thick crop of steel gray hair meticulously parted down the middle. His smooth face was covered with a neatly trimmed beard that was darker than his hair, giving him an imposing, sartorial look. Despite his advanced years, he was hale and hearty; in size and spirit. As the elder statesman of the group, he viewed himself as the leader of the Duluth Venture Club. The other members, all much younger, playfully referred to him as the 'old man'. But to their way of thinking, he had reached the pinnacle, and served as their model of what they hoped to accomplish in their lives.

Comstock-Peterson Logging, or C-P as it was known around the Arrowhead, was a well established timber concern that had moved into northeastern Minnesota twenty years earlier. As it had done in Maine, and later in the upper peninsula of Michigan, the company prospered by acquiring large tracts of public land, laying down temporary rail lines, and cutting all the merchantable timber it could find. Once done, the company would move on, letting the land, now stripped of its riches, go back to the counties on a tax forfeited basis. By controlling the wood supply, the rail lines, and the voracious sawmills that would soon line the Duluth harbor, C-P soon became one of the most prosperous businesses in the upper Midwest.

Peterson swayed slightly as he stood under the blue glow of a hissing gaslight chandelier, swishing the richly amber cognac in a Waterford lead crystal glass, a stub of a cigar clutched tightly in his other hand.

"Men, my logging foreman tells me I own a parcel of land." Peterson stopped for a moment and smiled to himself. "In fact I own hundreds, but this one

16

had few pine and was so remote, that it was not logged. For business purposes it is of little value, but it contains three fine lakes of some note. I propose that we locate and build a wilderness camp on the site, for the general good of all." He lifted the crystal glass high above his head, as if making an offering to the gods. "What do you say, men?"

At previous gatherings, members sometimes wistfully suggested that true men must test their mettle not only in the business world, but in the natural one as well. But until this moment, it had been nothing but idle talk. Now flushed with 25 year old cognac, the group spoke with a single voice, embracing the challenge. Soon ideas flowed and gurgled like the tumbling waters of the many North Shore rivers that the Club would need to cross to reach their new camp.

Chapter 3

As he lay clinging to the rotting tree stump like a life preserver in stormy seas, the commotion abruptly ceased. For a few anxious seconds Martin remained plastered to the ground before finally summoning the courage to cautiously peek over the top of the stump.

There in a small opening less than thirty feet away stood an enormous bull moose. Seemingly, unaware or likely unperturbed by Martin's presence, the huge beast with its poor eyesight and sharp sense of smell, pivoted its head and enormous antlers from side to side, trying to discover what its nose told him was lurking nearby. Fortunately for Martin, after several futile minutes, the moose wandered back into the brush, leaving behind a path of mangled stems and limbs. Shaken, but relieved, Martin coaxed himself upright, determined to finish the arduous journey that he had begun so early that morning.

*　　　　*　　　　*

The first hints of dull sunlight had barely tinted the sky over the Duluth harbor when Martin boarded a car of the Lake Front line at the Duluth train depot on this frosty late October morning in 1923. The train ran twice each day, covering a 30 mile stretch between Duluth and the busy rail hub of Knife River, located north and east of the city. As he stared blankly out the window, Martin could barely make out the churning waters of Lake Superior due to the heavy fog; a product of the warmer air from the highlands that surround Duluth crashing into the icy air that rose from the cold waters of the great lake.

Perched on one of the hard, pine benches worn smooth by a thousand before him, the train car rocked methodically as it traced the craggy shoreline of the lake. Only the occasional jostle from a frost-heaved rail joint broke the rhythmic clack of steel wheel on iron rail. The train's wood-fired boiler produced thick billows of dark gray smoke that floated peacefully out over the lake. The car was nearly filled with fellow travelers, speaking a variety of languages, but Martin noticed little as he busied himself studying the map and the letter that he had received from his brother.

Once the train arrived at the Knife River station, Martin engaged a motorcar service that had recently replaced ox and cart transportation, plying the slowly developing roadway between Knife River and the small towns scattered along the north shore of the lake. Earlier that year, the Duluth and Northern Minnesota Railroad had pulled up track that had originally traveled north and east from Knife River, and in doing so, marooned a string of small logging towns that were born when the timber and jobs were abundant. Now, access to Tettegouche Camp was much longer and more difficult.

Martin would endure almost two hours of head pounding travel on the narrow, rutted gravel road, until the motorcar pulled to a grinding stop next to a large weathered sign that announced:

Beaver Bay, Minnesota, Est. 1856

Though it served as the county seat of Lake County, it was a tiny village of sturdy souls who clung tenaciously to the craggy shoreline that surrounded the bay at the mouth of the Beaver River. Stout, grey, weather-beaten wooden structures formed a town that stoically displayed the effects of the sometimes fierce, always unpredictable weather that rolled off the cold waters of Lake Superior. Small fishing vessels, seemingly overmatched by the size and frequent intensity of the lake, lined the rugged pier that provided safe harbor for the boats, and the residents who depended on them for their very existence.

After thanking and paying the driver, Martin slung the heavy pack over his shoulder. The weight of the shiny green canvas backpack suddenly made him feel completely unprepared for the challenges and dangers that a ten mile trek through rugged, unmarked wilderness presented. But as he stepped from the car, he resolutely slung it over his shoulders, and set out with a determined stride.

As described in the map, he went straight up Birch Street which quickly changed from a two lane, hard surface roadway, to a narrow gravel road, and then into a well worn foot path, all within a half mile distance.   From there, the road-turned-trail climbed straight up the steep hill, one of many that separate the inland area of the Superior highlands region, from the rocky coast of Lake Superior.

Martin attempted to follow a trail had been hacked through the trackless wilderness in the 1860's by gold prospectors in search of Minnesota pay dirt. At one time the trail stretched all the way to the Canadian border. Now, in many places it had been swallowed up by thick vegetation, offering just an occasional hint of its former existence. Once he reached a lake, shown as

Bear Lake on his map, he would leave the trail completely, and bushwhack through the dense forest, now mostly inhabited by deer, moose, bear, and an occasional buckskin-clad fur trapper. Backed by a compass, his map, and cautious determination, he entered the heart of the Minnesota wilderness to find Tettegouche Camp, his brother Matts, and the reason for his mysterious letter.

Chapter 4

During the summer and fall of 1910, a construction crew operating out of the tiny logging village of Lax Lake located along the Duluth and Northern Minnesota Rail Line built a lodge, two sleeping quarters, and a horse stable all on a narrow strip of land along the shore of Micmac Lake. Nearby lay Tettegouche and Nipisquit lakes. The lakes were deep and pure despite the faint brownish color created by the tannins leached from the surrounding vegetation.

The white man names for these lakes had traveled with the loggers who arrived from New Brunswick, in eastern Canada. Micmac was a tortured translation of M'ikmaq, the name of a first nation tribe located along the far northeastern coast of North America. Nipisiquit was likely named after the Nepisiquit River in New Brunswick, and Tettegouche was a French term that literally translated as 'head west'.

It was beautifully rugged country, laced with short, steep hills littered with the rocky remains of glaciers long departed. A railroad grade carved into bedrock offered access to the area by providing firm footing for the rickety rail spur that had relentlessly hauled the lumberjacks and equipment in, and the last of the white pine out. After the 'jacks' work was done, the rails and ties had been pulled up to be used further up the line. That chiseled railroad bed would soon provide the rough and rocky entrance to Tettegouche Camp, the future wilderness retreat of the Duluth Venture Club.

By June of 1911 the Camp was finished and the charter members of the Venture Club made plans to christen the establishment with an elaborate party. Leaving their wives and mistresses behind, Arlo Peterson and the other six members, plus four women companions boarded one of Alan Prescott's best railcars, and set off along the rocking rail line that meandered through the forestland of northeastern Minnesota.

Prescott was of small frame with a head of chocolate brown hair and a thick beard to match. He had been born in Belfast, Ireland where his family lived in the shadow, soot, and soil of its bustling shipyards. His father was a well-respected construction foreman for Harland and Wolff, master shipbuilders for the White Star Line. In 1899, Alan marked his 18th birthday by following his wanderlust. On a cold, overcast morning he boarded White Star's newest, and the world's largest passenger ship, the RMS *Oceanic*, bound for New York City. Impatient and eager to chart his own way, he barely noticed the outstretched arm of Lady Liberty as he entered New York's teeming harbor on an icy December day.

A cousin, Gustav Prescott, a fair, hardworking sort, had discovered good fortune in a growing ship building business in Manitowoc, Wisconsin. Gustav, hoping that some of his uncle's qualities of industry and innovation had been borne into his cousin, offered the young Prescott a job. The economic depression that had afflicted many parts of the United States for the last decade was beginning to wane, and business was now booming.

Prescott, known as Scottie to his new business associates due to his name, and an inaccurate reference to his nationality, was determined to fulfill his bountiful ambition of being wealthy and powerful in his new land. Ethics and fair play were, from Scottie's perspective, obstacles to be overcome. He labored diligently to insure that such niceties would not stand in his way. A year after Scottie's arrival in Wisconsin, Gustav discovered that his cousin had been tuning up the company's financial ledgers to increase his slice of the pie. Their partnership was abruptly and acrimoniously terminated. With a pocket full of 'take this and get out' money, Prescott drifted north to the growing shipping center at the head of the great lakes, Duluth, Minnesota.

With a fine deep water harbor, and access to apparently infinite amounts of exploitable natural resources, Duluth was booming. Within just a couple of decades, Duluth had become a beacon for entrepreneurs and money men from across the country. By 1910, the Port of Duluth was handling more tons of cargo than any city in America, surpassing both New York and Chicago.

There, with some timely luck and his ill-gotten seed money Scottie entered the railroad business. He found a willing and useful partner in Thomas Schmidt, a displaced German businessman, with whom he formed the Duluth and Northern Minnesota Railroad. Within a year, the partners had taken over two smaller rail companies and quickly developed a very lucrative line that ran from the yards of Duluth, to its eventual northern terminus at Brule Lake, near the Canadian border. Soon a steady stream of workers and commerce were heading back and forth along D&NMR's ever expanding rail lines.

Around Duluth, Scottie became known for his fine clothing, smooth style, and unpredictable personality. Those who came to know him, found a bitter cherry in the middle of a chocolate confectionary. He could be courteous and generous when it furthered his needs; cold and calculating when it didn't. He was quick to anger and wildly unpredictable. Once, he struck one of his associates with his large, diamond willow walking cane simply for yelling at a dog. But his money and ambition made him a natural member of the Duluth Venture Club.

Schmidt, on the other hand, was quiet and intense, preferring to focus his energy on making deals and accumulating wealth. His personality, if there was one, could only be described as sullen, secretive and silent. He was willow thin, with a heavy brown mustache, and thick eyebrows that shaded his dark green eyes. He was very comfortable letting Scottie be the front man, while he worked tirelessly in the background to insure that whatever needed to happen, did.

As the train chugged its way north and east, Arlo Peterson kept up a steady patter describing the various land deals he had engineered as the train meandered through the scarred landscape that he had created. Peterson had spent his entire life in the timber business, acquiring and liquidating all the available white pine and merchantable hardwoods throughout the northeastern United States. Arriving in Duluth in 1897, he joined the timber rush that was quickly moving up the north shore, all the way to the Canadian border.

When the train finally arrived at the tiny Lax Lake station, two sturdy, heavily loaded wagons, each with a muscular pair of horses were waiting to transport the men and their female consorts to the camp. The cook, a Finn named Einar, grabbed the reins of one team, while Ben, who Peterson had hired as camp caretaker, grabbed the other.

Now as they wound their way toward the camp, the two men held their teams tightly, as the horses skillfully picked their way along the grade. Even so, the wagons jumped and bumped over the rocky tailings of the rail bed. The stout wood and steel wheels protested and groaned as they climbed up and over exposed bedrock and downed trees. After an hour long, jaw jarring ride the group arrived at the newly completed Tettegouche Camp. In addition to the seven members of the Club, the caretaker, the cook, and four women whom Peterson referred to as the 'auxiliary' completed that inaugural trip into Tettegouche Camp.

While several members of the Venture Club quietly referred to the woman as "those whores", the more charitable members preferred to think of them as business associates; providing the men with the services they desired in exchange for what the women needed, including stylish clothes, a decent place to live, and enough spending money to get by.

Now standing proudly at the front door of the impressive new lodge, Peterson spoke loudly, in his deep booming voice. "We shall find our time here to be one that we will remember," Peterson prophesized, and once the wagons were unloaded, the celebration began.

Chapter 5

Martin continued to claw his way through the dog's hair. As he sucked in lungs full of cool fresh air, he felt a slight breeze against his reddened check that carried the faint odor of wood smoke. He must be getting close. Now reenergized, he collected his wits, hitched up his load, and began what he hoped would be his final push toward the Camp. As he swam through the brush, the sweet smell of wood smoke grew stronger, and then, gratefully, the dog's hair began to thin as small groups of enormous white pine began to appear around him. A few minutes later, the outline of Tettegouche Camp appeared like a milky-white mirage. He had made it.

Slowly, he approached the main lodge. It was stout, two stories high, crafted with the finest of the enormous white pine that had taken seed in the area hundreds of years earlier. A tidy row of box windows ran across the long sides of the building about half way up the imposing walls; purposely placed high to allow light to bathe the interior of the building. Even now, the craftsmanship and care of construction was obvious, but the general condition of the building was depressing. Cedar shingles were missing or cracked, and moss was slowly enveloping the north side of the building.

Behind the lodge, clinging tightly to the shoreline of MicMac Lake were two other log structures in even more deplorable condition. Martin guessed them to be some sort of bunk houses. As he neared the lodge, he saw curly wisps of white smoke leaking from the blackened stone chimney. Wasting no time, he stepped up to the rough hewn door of the lodge and announced his presence by pounding it with his fist.

"Matts, it's me. Open up." Martin's voice was full and clear, and echoed through the woods around him. He paused, straining his ears for any reply. None came. He grabbed the door's rusty iron hasp, lifted it firmly and leaned heavily into the door. Creaking and groaning, it reluctantly swung open. The room was dark and shadowy, as he tiptoed cautiously into it. The great room received its only light from the small windows and the slowly dying fire in the enormous fireplace; a proud structure built with massive split stones that supported an equally massive quarter sawn log mantle. The fireplace nearly enveloped that side of the building scaling to the very top of the gable end of the lodge.

Within its hearth, a few cherry red embers cast a faint yellow glow across the room. With each flicker, shadows danced across the smooth dark walls. A moldy, smoky odor pieced his nostrils as he edged quietly toward the middle of the spacious room. The only sound was the mournful creak of the wood floor boards. Almost fearing an answer Martin called softly. "Matts, it's me." Again, the answer was silence.

In the dim light, he surveyed the surroundings. A heavy pine table, with several battered chairs sat desolately in the middle of the room. On either side of the fireplace hung a moose head, each with a magnificent set of antlers, the fur now tattered and careworn. Beneath one of the mounts, was a small table that held a kerosene lamp. Lying in front of the hearth was a filthy old mattress topped with several moth-eaten blankets. Inexplicably, next to these coarse, primitive

28

pieces stood what appeared to be a fine Victorian pressed back rocker.

Finding a box of matches on the mantle, he lit several of the kerosene lamps that hung on the wall; their glass chimneys blackened from heavy use and neglect. Stirring up the glowing embers in the fireplace, he tossed several craggy pieces of birch firewood onto the heap of coals. The crispy bark crackled and sparkled, and the dark lodge took on the somber look of a well-lit cave.

It was now obvious that the lodge was empty. "Where is Matts?" Martin wondered; not realizing he had spoken out loud until his voice echoed back to him. Other than the main entrance, the only other doorway into the great room led to a kitchen area. Constructed as an annex to the main building, Martin found a large iron sink and hand pump, and an enormous cast iron cook stove shoved up against the outside wall; on the interior wall hung a row of sturdy, well-crafted cupboards. A stout butcher block table with several more rough pine chairs stood in the middle. A single, four pane window, located directly above the sink, provided the only outside light.

While Martin was anxious to search the area for his brother, darkness had settled into the hills and forests that surrounded the lodge. Though a novice, he was wise enough to recognize the imprudence of wandering through a dense, unfamiliar forest with only starlight to guide him. He busied himself lighting several more of the kerosene lamps that clung to the heavy dark logs. The dirty wicks gave off a pungent, oily black smoke, and just enough light to cast dark shadows over the once proud kitchen

As he stared out the window toward MicMac Lake, a burning ache in his stomach reminded him that it

29

had been ten hours and 100 difficult miles since he had last eaten. Digging into his bulging backpack he retrieved some hard bread and sliced meat that he had carefully wrapped in waxed paper that morning. Gingerly testing the hand pump, he found it to be in working order. He filled a dingy glass with rust-colored water and washed down the dry sandwich. The aftertaste was mostly iron.

With the ache in his stomach satisfied, he considered his next move. "What I really need is sleep" he announced to the flies that were now buzzing around the crusty remains of his supper. Tomorrow would be soon enough to search for signs or clues of his brother's whereabouts.

Idly, he began to open and close the cupboards that lined the long interior wall of the kitchen. Most were empty, except for the nearly continuous layer of mouse droppings that littered the bottom of each cabinet, and nearly every shelf. Here and there he found a rusted tin plate, or chipped coffee cup. Surprisingly, in one cabinet he found a neat row of canned salmon and several wooden boxes of saltine crackers.

Reaching the last cupboard door, he pulled on it expecting it, like the others, to swing open with a rusty groan. Despite his efforts, the door would not budge. Carefully studying the front, sides and bottom, he discovered a small wooden latch placed out of sight, well beneath the cupboard. Giving it a quick pull, the bottom of the cabinet popped open. Martin jumped back startled, as if a ghost or wild animal would spring at him. Gratefully, if somehow disappointedly, all he found was a thick sheaf papers, tied neatly together with twine.

Curious, he positioned himself in one of the rickety chairs underneath the nearest lamp, intending to look through the sheaf of papers, when he heard a loud 'clunk' on the other side of the wall. Jerking his body around, he nearly tipped off his chair. His heart began pounding, and for a moment he strained to catch his breath. Cautiously, he raised himself from the chair, and tiptoed back into the great room. No hint of sunlight remained, and the darkness inside the lodge was nearly suffocating. With a soft trembling voice Martin called out. "Matts, is that you?"

Suddenly, the heavy lodge door blew open like it had been rigged with dynamite. In charged a burly, wildly unkempt man toting a double-barreled shotgun which he now leveled directly at Martin's head.

"Whadda you doing here?" the man growled. In that moment it occurred to Martin that if he could not provide an acceptable answer to that question, it would likely be his last worldly act.

Chapter 6

The following year, in July, 1912 the club members gathered for what was to be their biggest and best exploit of that summer. By this time, Prescott and Schmidt were finding their uneasy partnership unraveling like the seams of a poorly tailored suit. Schmidt, as intense and focused as ever, had begun to patently resent Scottie, who spent most of his time socializing and casually exhausting the fortunes that Schmidt worked so hard to accumulate. It was during the first night of the anticipated three day 'adventure' that the cork was forced from the bottle.

As evening settled over the Camp, Scottie sat in a corner of the lodge's great room with his feet slung over one of the large pine chairs, talking. As always, he spoke with a loud, brazen voice. "Schmidt, get me some more brandy," he instructed, shaking the empty glass like a hand bell. The German, who paid little heed to most people, conspicuously ignored him. "Schmidt, didn't you hear me? Bring me the bottle," Prescott hollered.

Again, Schmidt paid no attention, focusing instead on a business newspaper that he had carried with him from Duluth. Arlo Peterson and Billy O'Leary sat nearby, each with one of the town girls sitting on their laps.

O'Leary was a second generation Irishman. His grandparents, like so many of his countrymen, were driven from their native soil by the Great Famine that stuck Ireland in the mid 1850's. Living first in New York City, and later in Chicago, it was Billy's parents who came to Duluth seeking work. Billy was only thirteen when he took a job on one of the growing fleet of fishing boats operating out of the Duluth harbor. In an industry dominated by Finns and Swedes, Billy's willingness to work long hard hours in dangerous conditions made him a valuable asset, and within a couple years, he had saved enough money to buy his own boat and equipment. As the demand for lake trout, herring, and whitefish grew, so did O'Leary's fleet. By 1910, he had exchanged his smelly oil slickers and boots, for fancy, imported suits and shoes.

While the young Irishman now strenuously pawed at the girl, whose face displayed a pained look of bored resignation, Prescott launched the empty glass at Schmidt's head; missing his target but striking the girl sitting on O'Leary's lap flush in the mouth. The heavy glass split the girl's upper lip, loosened a couple of teeth, and caused a river of blood to cascade from the stunned girl's chin. She instinctively covered her face with her hands, sobbing.

Always a gentleman, even to those of the lower class, Schmidt leapt to his feet, and in three quick steps was across the room. His small bony hands encircled Scottie's thick neck. Though he was slight of build, it was clear that several years of accumulated frustration were giving Schmidt more strength than one would expect. If it weren't for the other members of the Venture Club coming to his rescue, it is possible that Scottie would have had his day of judgment that night.

After separating the two, an awkward silence fell over the room. Seething from the fiery exchange, Schmidt stormed from the lodge, slamming the heavy wooden door so hard that it rattled the windows. No one seemed too concerned, but a tense sullen mood descended over the partiers. More alcohol was drunk, and more stories told, but the festive mood that most had anticipated dripped away like the rivulets of blood that rained onto the girl's long gingham dress.

The following morning, long after the sun had found its way through the thick canopy of spruce and birch, the revelers began to stir. Peterson was the first to find his footing and slowly make his way to the lodge, hoping that the cook had started a pot of much needed coffee.

Gratefully he discovered that Einar had been busy; a large, blue porcelain coffee pot was gurgling on the cook stove, emitting a strong, pleasant aroma. As the sunlight of the bright July morning streamed through the kitchen window, Peterson fed several pieces of firewood into the stove, and poured himself a steaming cup of black coffee. As he carefully sipped the tongue-scalding brew, Peterson glanced outside. Against the backdrop of the mirror flat waters of MicMac Lake, Peterson spotted Scottie walking quickly along the shore. He appeared to be in a single-minded hurry, slinking through the brush and downed trees. Soon he vanished from sight.

As the sun rose higher into a cloudless powder blue sky, its powerful rays began to burn off the morning fog that formed and drifted between the cool lake waters. Billy O'Leary wandered out of his sleeping alcove, eager to roust the others. "Time to rise you lazy lads," he hollered down the narrow corridor that connected the sleeping alcoves. His lighthearted greeting was met with grumbles and grunts.

As O'Leary moved through the sleeping quarters, it was apparent that Ben the caretaker had dutifully loaded and fired the large Round Oak 20 wood stove located at the far end of the hall. It was glowing dark orange, filling the sleeping quarters with a welcome wave of heat. Though it was summer in northeastern Minnesota, cool Canadian air often found its way south making early summer feel like late fall.

Slowly, other members of the Venture Club began to stir. All were groggy, feeling the affects of the long night. Andersen padded slowly out of his room, joining O'Leary and Anders Johnson around the woodstove. "Where are the others?" Andersen asked as he stood close to the stove while rubbing his hands together.

Johnson, a usually cheery and boisterous sort found a brain splitting hangover clouding his mood. "How should I know," he spouted, a bit annoyed that anyone would think that he cared where the others were.

"Let's go over to the lodge. Breakfast should be ready by now," O'Leary suggested. "I really need a cup of the brew."

As the three made their way from the sleeping quarters, they saw Alan Prescott dart from the dense wooded area west of the camp heading in the direction of the lodge. Andersen called out. "Scottie, where have you been?"

Prescott did not answer, but silently ducked into the side door of the lodge. As the club members gathered in the kitchen, Arlo Peterson gazed at the pale, tired faces; all except for Prescott's, whose skin was flushed, dotted with small beads of sweat glistening on his forehead. "Prescott, what have you been up to?" Peterson inquired caustically. "Been over to the girls' cabin already this morning?" He let out a snort, thinking on one hand the depravity that Scottie could display, and on the other a bit of reluctant jealousy for his perceived vigor.

"I went out for a walk; needed to clear my head," Prescott responded, his voice sinking to a whisper as he spoke the word 'head'.

Ben, the caretaker, was filling the cook stove, with small chunks of split birch. He seemed to pay little attention to the men gathered in the kitchen. When he had finished his chores in the kitchen, he headed out into the great room to begin cleaning up the remains of the previous night.

Looking around, Peterson noticed that one of their group was missing. "Where is Schmidt?' Peterson asked, staring directly at Scottie.

Feeling Peterson's steely gaze, Scottie shot back, "How would I know. You saw him stomp out last night. He probably went back to the bunk room. If he's not in his bed, he's probably out in the woods… somewhere."

Peterson found Prescott's explanation unsatisfactory. He was still troubled by the fight that had broken out between the two the previous night. He was also aware that their partnership was disintegrating for reasons he did not fully understand. "If he's not back by the time we get some coffee and food in our bellies, we're going to look for him," Peterson declared.

Einar had prepared a heavy breakfast of bacon, ham, fried potatoes and pancakes and the men ate their fill with barely a word being spoken. An hour later, there was still no sign of Schmidt. The sun was now directly overhead, and reluctantly the six men headed out to locate the missing German. Peterson took charge, directing the men to insure a methodical search.

"Andersen and Prescott you go round the north side of Micmac. If you locate him, fire a shot, and we will meet back here. O'Leary and Johnson you head over to Nipisiquit and do the same. Wentworth and I will check the area over by Tettegouche."

John Wentworth was the newest member of the Adventure Club. Though still in his twenties, he had quickly established a reputation as a ruthless, relentless barrister willing to take on the most unsavory of cases, and notorious of clients. Slight of build, with straight, ebony-colored hair, he looked even younger than his age would suggest, leading some of the veteran prosecutors in Duluth to dismiss 'the boy' as someone they could intimidate and push around the court room. They would soon learn that young Mr. Wentworth was not a man to trifle with. Bright and diligent, he demonstrated a ready willingness to do whatever necessary to insure his clients were well treated by the court system. His devotion to hard work and winning tough cases had already made him one of the richest lawyers in Duluth. Peterson, who had used Wentworth's services on several occasions, appreciated those qualities in the young man, and had recently invited him to join the Venture Club.

As he and Peterson make the short trek toward Tettegouche Lake, Wentworth toyed with a finely engraved, chrome plated .45 caliber pistol, a Colt Peacemaker, he had purchased just before coming to the Camp. He had never actually fired a handgun before, but he liked the feel and supreme sense of power such a deadly weapon slung from his waist provided. He had worn it everywhere since he had arrived at camp. While many of his clients were well-versed in the power and possibilities such a handgun could provide, for Wentworth it was a shiny new toy.

As he aimlessly followed Peterson through the brush, he envisioned himself being the object of a ferocious black bear attack. The man-eating creature with jaws snapping would leap from behind one of the enormous boulders that were scattered randomly along the shoreline of the pristine lake. Spotting the creature, he would react with lightening quickness; just like the western lawmen he read about in the dime novels on the bookshelves in his office, and drop the beast with a single, well-placed bullet to the head.

"John come here now!" Peterson's voice echoed through the still air, each word forming a sentence.

The urgency in Arlo's voice snapped Wentworth from his daydream. Up ahead, Peterson was standing at the water's edge, staring out toward a small patch of bright green cattails standing tall in the shallow water, twenty feet from shore. Nervously, Wentworth's right hand encircled the ivory grip of his pistol, as he hurried to join Peterson. Arlo now raised his arm and pointed toward the cattails. "Look there!"

As Wentworth's eyes followed the direction Peterson was pointing, he tried to comprehend what was floating so placidly in the clear waters of the lake. But the interwoven bands of shadows and light made it difficult for Wentworth to decipher what he was seeing. "What is that?" Wentworth queried Peterson as he watched the object bob slowly up and down in the tranquil waters of Tettegouche Lake.

"I'm pretty sure it's Schmidt," Peterson replied firmly.

Chapter 7

As Martin continued to stare down the muzzles of the double-barreled shotgun he was frozen with fear, "Who are you?" the man growled again, as the shotgun now wavered just a few feet from his face.

"I am Martin Andersen...I'm a doctor... in Duluth...I came here to find my brother…..….. He sent me a letter…….." Martin spoke so fast the words came out in one breath.

The man with the gun edged closer, straining his eyes to make out Martin's profile in the dimly lit lodge. His dirty red hair and beard were nearly contiguous around his head, and it was obvious neither had seen a scissor, comb or lye soap for a very long time. He wore a filthy wool shirt that hung down to the middle of his thighs, covering a ragged pair of buckskin britches. As he slid closer, the yawning barrels of the shotgun were now just inches from Martin's forehead.

"A doctor?   Who you lookin'fer?"

"Matts Andersen, my brother, please believe me," Martin pleaded. "Why else would I come out to this old lodge in the middle of the wilderness?" Martin hoped that simple logic would encourage the man to lower his long gun who was now so close that Martin could smell him; a putrid combination of dirt and sweat that affronted his nose.

Suddenly, an unexpected look of comprehension washed over the man's face. "How long," he asked with a skeptical tone, "since ya seen him?" He let the shotgun barrel dip slowly. Martin exhaled for the first time in what seemed like hours.

"It has been more than ten years," Martin replied.

"Well, I ain't seen him for that long neither," the man chortled, as his eerie laugh echoed through the empty lodge.

Martin was dumbfounded by the man's odd response, and wondered if he was addled; a lunatic, or maybe a heinous criminal on the run. "Please, mister, put down the gun, and let's talk. I'm didn't come here to bother you, and the sooner we talk, the better it will be for both of us." Martin was scared, confused, and unsure of what to do next. But the mounting affects of the grueling day were creating a sense of exasperation that was gaining the upper hand on fear.

The wild man's dark brown eyes stared fiercely into Martin's, and then unexpectedly, he laid down his gun on the rough hewn pine table. More surprisingly, he smiled and offered Martin his hand. "I'm Benjamin Stock...born in Beaver Bay....been living in this old lodge for more'n three years now....ever since my wife Lorraine ran off with another man." His voice trailed off, and surprisingly his dark brown eyes filled with tears. Composing himself, he continued. "I hunt, and sell game in town. Do some fur trappin' to buy my essentials. This place is home." He talked in short, staccato sentences that said a lot without saying much.

"Have you seen anyone else around here recently?" Martin inquired, trying to fit the man's story with the letter that had brought him to this remote spot.

"Ever' so often, a lost hunter will stumble by. I give 'em directions. And there's the old Indian, White Feather, lives some miles south of here. He stops by

40

ever' so often. That's about all." Stock sounded very sure and convincing. Martin was now more perplexed and decided he needed to start at the beginning.

"How did you end up here, Mr. Stock?"

"Call me Sarge, everybody does," replied Stock as he idly gazed over Martin's shoulder toward the window that looked out over MicMac Lake. A sliver of moon had appeared, creating just enough light to cause the gentle ripples of the lake to dance across the surface, as the stars twinkled in the cloud-free sky. A faraway look in his eyes suggested that Stock was trying to conjure up the events that led him to Tettegouche Camp.

"I left Beaver Bay when I was 16, and moved to Lax Lake," he began. "Me and my Pap ran a livery stable there. It was mostly a logging town then. Pap and me kept horses for C-P". He spoke more slowly now, his voice tinged with just a trace of an eroded New England accent.

"The logging company?" Martin interjected.

"Yeh, that's right," Stock replied. "They pretty much owned everything and everybody in Lax Lake. Then in '17, I joined up...the army, spent almost two years in the war."

"But how did you end up here," Martin persisted, still trying to understand how the only person at Tettegouche Camp was not his brother, but a hermit with a gun.

"We provided horses for the Camp." Stock replied. "They spent a year hauling materials, putin' up these buildings...got to know the foreman pretty good. I guess he liked me. Once the camp was done, he offered me a job."

"A job at the camp?"

"Yep"

41

"Doing what?

"Caretaker," Stock replied slowly.

Caretaker? For several moments Martin stared at Sarge, trying to determine if this new bit of information might fill in any of the assorted gaps in the circumstances that had brought him to this place. It did not. He decided to take a different approach. Opening up the top of his backpack, he dug out the letter that had arrived at this office two days earlier.

"Mr. Stock, eh, Sarge, as I mentioned, my brother and I have not seen each other for over ten years," Andersen continued. "Though we are identical twins, we never had much in common, and then about ten years ago, what was left of our relationship ended."

"Yeh, sure I remember him some now. You two do look alike, 'cept I don't recall him having any chin whiskers. So what does the letter say?" Stock asked calmly, trying to bring the subject back to where it began. He could hardly imagine words so powerful and persuasive that they would inspire a city doctor to hike through ten miles of unmarked wilderness at the request of a brother he hadn't seen for a decade.

"Yes, the letter." Slowly and deliberately, Martin unfolded the thick notepaper and began to read.

Dear Martin, you are probably as surprised in receiving this letter as I am in writing it. I know we have never been close, but I am now in a situation where I must ask you to forget the past. My life is in mortal and imminent danger, and I can think of no other way to save it. Please, please you must come to Tettegouche Camp as soon as you receive this letter. Since they pulled up the tracks to Lax Lake, the only way to get here is by foot from Beaver Bay. I have drawn a map that will help you find it. I beg you to come as soon as you get this letter. I have nowhere else to turn.

Matts

Stock exhaled slowly, feeling the desperation in the words. "So you came," Stock began. "What did ya expect to find?"

Martin shrugged his shoulders. There were still many questions, but Stock, who was always direct, pulled on the thread of one of those nagging issues.

"Doc, what happened ten years ago between you two?" he asked Martin pointedly.

Martin looked straight into Stock's eyes and said without hesitation, "Mr. Stock, I am pretty sure that my brother was involved in a murder here at the Camp."

Chapter 8

Ka-boom. An ear piercing explosion erupted from the barrel of John Wentworth's Colt pistol reverberating across the water and echoing through the woods surrounding the Camp.

Wentworth was totally unprepared for the recoil such a powerful weapon generated, and was staggered backward, nearly tripping over a fallen log. Catching himself, he holstered his heavy sidearm and began to jog toward the lodge.

Wentworth was surprised, and a bit amazed how calm Arlo Peterson remained after discovering the body floating face down in the lake. Without hesitation, he had waded out into the shallow waters to insure that what he had found was what he had feared. Grabbing the shoulder of the corpse he lifted it up far enough to get a good look at the face of the victim. The skin of Schmidt's face and hands was a whitish blue, and Wentworth could see that Schmidt's body was well-stiffened from rigor mortis.

"Fire a shot, Wentworth," Peterson had instructed, "then go back and get the others."

As Wentworth trotted back along the trail, his lawyer instincts took over as he tried to unravel the situation. It could have been an accident, he told himself. Schmidt left in an agitated state. He had been drinking. He could have wandered into the water, fallen and drowned. But as he weighed the particulars more thoroughly, it began to gnaw at his guts that this may not have been an accident. In criminal law, attorneys are trained to consider three elements; motive, means and opportunity; the why and how often identifying the 'who'. Wentworth knew for certain that at least one of the Venture Club members possessed all three. Breathing hard from the run up the hill, his face flushed from the unexpected turn of events, Wentworth stepped into the side door of the lodge. Upon hearing the gunshot, the others were now heading in; relieved that such a needless 'goose chase' had ended so quickly.

"So what was the old bastard doing?" Billy O'Leary asked sarcastically, assuming Schmidt was out wandering in the woods, planning some sort of big deal, causing unneeded exertion for the other members of the Club.

"He's dead," Wentworth blurted out.

"What?' O'Leary shot back. "How?" The other members of the Venture Club stared at the young lawyer waiting for some sort of explanation. All eyes were focused on Wentworth, except one; Alan Prescott stood quietly behind the others, staring at his hands.

Before Wentworth could form a reasonable response to O'Leary's questions, he launched another.

"Where?"

"Floating face down in Tettegouche Lake," Wentworth offered meekly. "Peterson found him. He is dead, for sure. And from the stiffness of the body it appears he's been there quite a while. Peterson said we should all come, now, right now!"

Confused but compliant, the four men followed Wentworth back down the trail to the lake. No words were spoken as each man formed his own thoughts about what might have happened, and more importantly what to do about it. A fresh breeze was now rising from the west, flipping the leaves of the quaking aspens, creating a soft harmonious rustling sound. The last remains of the morning dew fell from the trees as they walked. After a short hike they arrived at the lake to find Peterson standing stoically, his arms folded in front of him. His face was dark, his expression grim.

"He's dead, been dead quite awhile from the looks of it," Peterson reported dispassionately. "Does anybody know anything about this?" His tone was more inquisitive than accusatory, but it immediately put the members on edge.

"What are you suggesting?" Prescott shot back. "Do you think one of us had something to do with this? This looks like an accident, plain and simple. He was drunk, wandered out in the dark by himself, tripped and fell into the lake."

Several others began to nod; hoping, wishing that Schmidt's death was nothing more than a regrettable accident. Otherwise, someone standing within yards of them was a murderer.

Chapter 9

Murder? Benjamin Stock was surprised not just by the words, but by the nonchalance with which Martin Andersen spoke them.

"Who do you think he.......?" Before Stock could finish forming his question, the proverbial scales fell from his eyes and several pieces, of the up to now indecipherable puzzle, began to slide together. "You think your brother killed that railroad man here at the Camp?" Stock stopped, and tugged at his beard as he considered something, that until this moment had never crossed his mind.

He ransacked his jumbled memory trying to recreate the scene and circumstances that occurred at the Camp so many years ago. Slowly and powerfully like the November waves of an angry Lake Superior storm crashing onto the rocky reefs surrounding Beaver Bay, he was jolted with the memory of that day. But just as quickly, he discovered a flaw in Martin's story.

"That man weren't murdered. He drowned. Me and the cook we fished him outta the lake. Everyone said he drowned." Sarge nodded, confident of his answer.

By this time, the flames in the large fireplace had burned low and deep shadows were returning to the room, casting an eerie pall over the two men. With a forlorn look, Martin Andersen stood up and slowly walked toward the fireplace. He grabbed several pieces of firewood from the wood box and tossed them gently on the mound of glowing embers. Immediately, the birch bark caught fire, and tongues of fire jumped from the dry wood sending waves of orange light into the room. Grabbing an iron poker that was leaning up against the wood box, Martin suddenly wheeled, and pointed it directly at the caretaker's face. "That man didn't drown and the girl didn't run off."

Chapter 10

Anders Johnson stood apart from the others as they milled along the shore of the lake. Though he had been a member for several years, he struggled to get a fair measure of the men of the Venture Club. Like them, he was filled with ambition and drive. But he was deeply troubled by their casual absence of conscience in their personal and professional lives. Now, the very real possibility that one of the men standing next to him was a murderer sent shivers through his body.

Johnson was a large man; portly was the polite adjective often used to describe men of his size and girth. He had a face as round as a basketball, with a shock of straight blond hair, and a droopy mustache he would often twirl between his fingers when talking to others. He had a ready laugh, and a self-deprecating attitude; a rare trait for a man of his power and social stature.

Johnson had immigrated to America in 1901, finding that good timing was leading to good fortune. In the old country, he had attended and graduated from the Goteborgs Universitet in Goteborg, Sweden. He excelled at engineering, honing a skill and uncovering a passion for designing bridges, railroads, and harbor installations. Sweden's economy at the turn of the century was at low ebb providing scant opportunity for a man of his training and talents. So when the stories relayed in letters from relatives living in America described streets of gold and fortunes for the taking, it took little prodding for Johnson to make the long journey to the new world.

Arriving in Duluth as the 20th century was dawning, Johnson found a city with a ravenous appetite for the type of projects he most enjoyed. And it would be one of his first efforts that would quickly become one of the city's most prominent landmarks; the Duluth Aerial Transfer Bridge.

Lying east of the St. Louis River estuary and running in a southerly direction is a narrow, seven mile long strip of land that separates Lake Superior from the back bays of Duluth and Superior, Wisconsin. Attached to the north shore immediately below the city of Duluth, the slender ribbon of land was known locally as Minnesota Point. The only natural passage through Minnesota Point lies on the far southern end near Superior, Wisconsin which provided that town an enviable shipping advantage that would soon be deemed wholly unsatisfactory by the residents of Duluth. They pledged to do something about it.

In 1870 Duluth city fathers combined forces with the Lake Superior and Mississippi Railroad to dig a channel on the north end of Minnesota Point. The passage, which was 245 wide and 28 feet deep, became known as the Duluth Ship Canal, providing easy access to the docks and piers in Duluth harbor.

Unfortunately for those living on Minnesota Point, they were now marooned on a long, willowy island. For thirty years, various methods were employed to transport residents back and forth; boats and ferries were common when the lake was ice-free, but when the harsh winds of Duluth's often interminable winter blew in, crossing the ship canal was a difficult and dangerous task.

In response, Johnson's company provided the plans and blueprints for the transfer bridge, which when completed stood astride the ship canal, towering 200 feet in the air, providing safe passage for man and machine across the ship canal. It was a marvel of human invention, and a bold new landmark in the Zenith City.

Now as Johnson and the other men stood silently along the shores of Tettegouche Lake, Peterson again took charge. "Johnson, go back to the lodge. Get the caretaker and cook to come retrieve the body." This was dirty, distasteful work, best done by the hired men. "The rest of us," Peterson instructed, "will wait here." To the other members of the Venture Club, whatever the cause of death, this situation needed to be cleaned up quickly and quietly. They all knew that dead bodies were not good for business.

Johnson huffed and panted making his way slowly up the hill. As he neared the buildings, he caught movement in one of the windows of the women's sleeping quarters. The smaller of the two cabins provided accommodations for the Duluth women who took residence and, sometimes refuge from the men, within its sturdy log walls. They were expected to be available when the club members needed them, yet invisible and out of the way, when they didn't.

As he got closer, he could see that one of the women, Sally, was leaning from the open window vigorously waving a towel, trying to attract his attention. While Anders was not immune to the favors the women provided, he always felt a sharp pang of guilt and sadness for the women's situation. He assured himself that their association with the Venture Club was their choice, and they received appropriate compensation for their services. But the arrangement still troubled him,

51

even when at times, their services did not.

Sally Keefe was tough Irish lassie with flaming red hair and a temperament to match. Johnson knew very little about her background, but was keenly aware that she was brash and outspoken, and extremely protective of 'her' girls. While she provided her services without fail, she was strong willed, and would, at times, stand up to the men when she felt they were expecting too much. She had grown up in Grand Rapids, Minnesota without a mother, who died shortly after bringing Sally into the world. At the age of 14, she was raped by her father. When Sally's protective older brother found out what had happened, her father ended up in the cemetery with a bullet in his head, and her brother landed in the Stillwater State Prison for putting it there. With no family to hold her, she took the cars from Grand Rapids to Duluth.

"Sally, what is it?" Johnson called up to the window as he neared the log building.

Sally stopped her frantic waving, and yelled back, "it's Hannah."

"What about her?" Johnson shot back.

"She's gone."

Chapter 11

After chewing on Martin's bold statement that there had been <u>two</u> murders at the Camp, Benjamin Stock began to wonder if the good doctor was daft. A man who claims to be a city doctor wanders into the middle of nowhere; looking for a brother he hasn't seen in a decade, claiming that two people were killed at the Camp for which Stock was the caretaker. 'What, if any, part of this fairy tale was he going to believe?' he wondered to himself.

"Martin, there weren't no woman killed here. As I recall, that one, she just up and left. And that railroad man drowned, pure and simple. And there ain't been no one here for four years or more. You sure about any of this?" Stock stared at Martin with a look of disbelief and pitiful compassion.

A mask of frustration appeared on the doctor's face as he was overcome by a bout of lightheadedness. Fatigue and confusion enveloped his mind in a thick, impenetrable fog. Once more he stared deeply into Stock's eyes searching for a hint of clarity; that what he was saying, that what he had come to believe so fervently, was in fact true.

"Mr. Stock, I told you that I am a doctor in Duluth, and that is absolutely true. I have a twin brother who was a member of the Duluth Venture Club, and that is also true." Drawing a deep breath, he paused for a moment. "Let me assure you that while they claimed that man drowned, and that the girl ran off, I am almost certain that both were murdered."

Benjamin Stock rocked back slowly in his Victorian chair, the only relic that provided a hint of the Camp's former rustic elegance. As he did, he ran his work worn hands through his shaggy crop of course reddish brown hair. His eyes slowly wandered up the thick walls of the lodge before landing on the massive ridgepole that ran the length of the building, bearing the weight of the entire roof structure. Stock was beginning to understand that Andersen was feeling much like that ridgepole as he worked to unwind the confusing and ominous details of what was happening.

As Stock rocked, Andersen got to his feet and frenetically began to pace the floor. He was past exhaustion, propelled by a sort of human kinetic energy. To Stock, the doctor's pacing reminded him of a grey wolf snared in a leg hold trap. "Mr. Stock, eh, Sarge, if you are agreeable, I would like to impose upon you for a night's rest in your…home. If I am going to sort this out, I need some rest."

Stock nodded his head agreeably. "Did'ya bring a bedroll? Lay it in front of the fireplace next to mine if you want." He pointed toward the tattered mattress and filthy pile of blankets that Andersen had noticed when he first entered the lodge. Andersen nodded as he opened his large backpack, and dug two neatly folded, colorful wool blankets and a shiny white pillow from the pack. A sympathetic toothy grin appeared on Stock's face as he shook his head. "Doc, you really are a city slicker, ain't ya?" he said with a kind, playful tone.

For the first time since leaving Duluth, Martin smiled a sheepish smile. A warm and welcome wave of relief washed over him as he carefully unfolded the new blankets and laid them neatly next to the split-stone raised hearth of the fireplace. When he was satisfied, he headed toward the kitchen to draw a glass of iron-edged water. His mouth was as dry as warm carded cotton and even foul water would taste good right now.

As he stepped through the entryway of the kitchen and approached the massive cast iron sink, one of the four panes of the large window that looked out over Micmac Lake imploded, and a whistling sound buzzed by his right ear. Shards of glass flew in his face, as he stumbled backward toward the doorway, falling flat on his back just as a second pane of glass exploded, showering him with more bits of glass. From the other room Stock's deep voice boomed.

"Doc!"

Dazed, but alert, Andersen could feel heavy footsteps as Stock sprang from his chair and ran toward the kitchen. Opening his eyes and staring up at the ceiling, he felt warm rivulets running down his cheek and forehead. With this right hand, he instinctively probed his face to wipe at the liquid. Holding his hand in front of his eyes, his fingers dripped red. 'How strange he thought to himself, my own blood'. A second later, Stock was on his hands and knees, his face hovering directly over Martin, exhaling his foul breath into Andersen's face. Stock's eyes were wide as saucers, displaying a look of bewilderment and fear.

"Are you shot?" Stock bellowed, beginning to understand what had happened in that split second.

"I don't know," Martin answered slowly. Taking several deep breaths, his medical training began to return, as he attempted to diagnose his condition. "Is there a hole?" Andersen asked with a tremor in his voice.

As an experienced hunter, Stock was very familiar with the appearance of entry and exit wounds in the animals he would shoot. Even to his untrained eye, these injuries did not look life threatening. "Looks like cuts to me... pretty sure just the glass got ya."

"I have a medical kit in my backpack. Get it," Andersen ordered.

Stock looked up at the two shattered window panes. It was clear that someone had fired twice at Andersen, both narrowly missing their mark. Stock did not intend to be the next target and kept well below the sill of the window as he slid out into the great room.

Digging blindly through Martin's pack, he felt something hard and heavy, neatly wrapped in a clean white towel. Unfolding the bundle, Stock discovered a Colt M1911; a military issue .45 caliber semi-automatic pistol. With its six inch rectangular barrel, coated in steel blue, the M1911 was standard issue to all American doughboys ranked sergeant and above during the Great War. Stock was well acquainted with the weapon. As a member of the Quartermaster Corps of 'Black Jack' Pershing's American Expeditionary Force, he had distributed caseloads of these side arms to the American boys heading for the trenches on the western front. It was the first pistol that reliably captured the energy of a fired bullet to chamber the next round. Its smooth action was capable of firing as fast as the shooter could pull the trigger. With a heavy rifled slug and a generous load of gunpowder, officers in the AEF often claimed that the pistol 'kicked like one of Black Jack's Army mules.' With a twelve cartridge clip that slipped neatly into the handle, it was a powerful killing machine.

Given the events of the last few minutes, his discovery of this formidable weapon, wrapped up in a neat white bundle, made Stock wonder if there was more going on than one brother's cry for help?

"Did you find it," Andersen yelled from where he lay in the doorway. He tried to calm himself, just as he would his injured and frightened patients, but the blood, the pain and uncertainty of what was happening was making that nearly impossible.

"Yah, got it," Stock shouted as he grabbed a metal box marked with a red cross and crawled quickly back toward Andersen. By now the flow of blood had eased, as the wounds were not deep. At Andersen's direction, Stock examined each of the cuts for traces of glass; happy to inform Martin that none appeared. Opening a small bottle of alcohol from the medical kit, Stock swabbed the blood from the wounds, and clumsily taped strips of linen gauze over each of them. When he finished, Andersen looked a little like an Egyptian mummy.

For a brief moment, the soft crackling of the smoldering birch firewood made the only sounds. But in that moment it became uncomfortably clear to both men that whoever had fired those shots was still out there. And while the attacker might not be certain if one or both shots found their target, it was very likely he would be determined to find out.

Stock feverish snaked across the kitchen floor toward the kitchen's exterior door. Once there, he reached up and engaged the sturdy deadbolt lock. He then placed the heavy interior door brace in its iron bracket; a security improvement that Stock had installed after a determined black bear had defeated the deadbolt and ransacked the kitchen back in 1911.

Meanwhile, Martin had wobbled to his feet. Staying away from the shattered window, he extinguished the kerosene lanterns along the kitchen wall. Soon it was as dark inside the kitchen as it was outside. Remembering that the main door was not properly secured, Stock jumped to his feet eager to remedy that situation. For just a brief second his body formed a faint shadow in the doorway visible through the shattered glass window. The 'psst' of a streaking bullet, followed by a loud report, and a splintering of glass and wood happened in an instant.

The bullet chewed into the doorframe just over Stock's head, showering him with ragged slivers of wood. The instincts of an old soldier returned, and he dropped to his belly, using his elbows and knees to slither lizard-like across the floor. In a few seconds, he reached the main door, which he defiantly locked and secured. Rolling on this back, he lay still as a stone, with only his heaving chest making any movement at all.

And then, nothing; but the soft murmur of the slowly burning fire.

Chapter 12

S till trying to catch his breath from his trip up the hill, Johnson placed his hands on his hips while sucking in the warm summer air. After a minute or so, he cocked his head back, and stared up at Sally as he tried to make sense of what she had just told him. He was now standing directly under the window, his head tilted back, staring into Sally's intense green eyes. The brilliant sun hovering almost directly above her, forced Johnson to shield his eyes.

"What do you mean she's gone? Are you sure?"

"Late in the night, well after the lodge was quiet, Mr. Schmidt come calling. He told me he wanted Hannah to go with him." Sally was speaking so fast her words ran together as she relayed the story. "I told Schmidt it was too late, that everyone was tired, and that he should just go to bed."

She stopped for a moment while slowly whisking away some of the soft red curls that had fallen in front of her eyes. Johnson could tell from the look on Sally's face and earnest tone to her voice that she was telling the truth. "Mr. Schmidt insisted. He told me that he just wanted to go for a walk and that he would have her back in a short while. She never came back."

"Sally, they just found Schmidt floating face down in the lake. He's dead."

She stared down at Johnson, with a look of disbelief. "They don't think Hannah did it, do they?" She stopped

59

and gazed toward the lake. "If they do, she probably had every right. He was a terrible man."

After an eerie moment of silence, Johnson remembered his real mission. Leaving Sally with a dumbfounded look on her face, he trotted toward the lodge. Slipping in the side door, he found the cook and caretaker sitting quietly at the large butcher block table sipping cups of coffee.

"Come with me!" Johnson huffed, his mouth wide open as he again tried to catch his breath. He was now panting as he relayed Peterson's directions. "Schmidt is dead.... in the lake.....must have drowned last night..... Peterson wants you to come......retrieve the body."

The cook, Einar Toivinen looked at the caretaker with a confused expression. Einar spoke little English, and was not sure what Johnson had just told them. However, from the tone of the Swede's voice and the twisted expression that now seized Stock's face, he knew it was bad. Ben, who had spent much of youth among the Finnish immigrants of Beaver Bay, had developed a working knowledge of their language.

He turned to Toivinen, "Schmidt is dead, he's 'on kuollut'." Stock waved his hand, indicating that Einar should follow him.

Reluctantly, they rose from their comfortable spots, heading out to the supply shed to see what they could find. Locating a couple of stout pine posts and several heavy wool horse blankets and ropes, they were able to fashion a crude but functional stretcher. Following Johnson, they headed back down the rocky trail to the lake.

As they neared the group standing along the shore, they could hear and see that the members of the Venture Club were engaged in a heated quarrel.

Wentworth, the lawyer, was making a legal sounding argument for what he considered the appropriate action to take. "We need to take the body to Lax Lake, and report the death to the county sheriff," he said declared firmly.

Peterson and several of the others nodded slowly as they listened to Wentworth's advice, until Alan Prescott interrupted the conversation. "The man is dead," he stated bluntly as his piercing brown eyes took on a look that married anger and fear. "How he died is of no real concern to us. I say we weigh the body with stones and sink it in the lake. When we get back to town, we just report that he decided to head back early, and that is all we know." He stopped as suddenly as he had started, creating an awkward silence. After several seconds Billy O'Leary, his face now red as blood, spoke the words the others were thinking.

"You killed him, you bastard, you killed him," he yelled while stabbing a stubby finger directly in Prescott's face. "You followed him when he left the lodge and clubbed him with a stone or log before tossing his body in the lake."

O'Leary wiped his mouth with the back of sleeve while contemplating the harsh words that had just burst from his lips. He had surprised himself with his fierce tone; almost like a cornered timber wolf facing off with a black bear. He had never liked Scottie, not one bit. Such a heinous act was not surprising and he just spoke what he believed to be true.

Peterson now caught a glimpse of Johnson and the hired men approaching and waved his hand. All fell silent. This conversation would continue, but it was for Venture Club member ears only, and they all knew it. Whether they realized it or not, their fate was now strung together like a team of horses pulling a wagon loaded heavy with field stones.

Again Peterson took charge. He turned and pointed toward the small cluster of cattails. Though he spoke directly to the hired men, he was intent on speaking for all the members of the Venture Club. "It appears our friend Mr. Schmidt met with an unfortunate accident last night. We are all deeply saddened by this turn of events. We must gather up his body and report this situation to the authorities."

Still fuming, O'Leary turned toward Prescott, who, feeling the Irishman's icy stare looked idly at the ground. 'This ain't over yet' O'Leary thought to himself. Just then, a westerly breeze began to freshen dramatically, and energetic waves began to lash the rocky shoreline. Then, as if guided by some mystic force, Schmidt's body broke free from its entanglement with the cattails and began to float slowly toward shore.

Einar and Ben waded cautiously into the cool water. The lake bottom was slippery, coated with slimy silt and decaying leaves. Once out to where the body now bobbed in the lake, each grabbed one of Schmidt's ankles, and began to drag the corpse toward shore. They wasted no time completing their disdainful chore. Once there, they flipped the body over and placed Schmidt's earthly remains onto their improvised stretcher. Water dripped from his face and hair, and his waterlogged clothes clung tightly to his lifeless form. His eyes were wide open, now staring at the sky and the heavens above. The skin of his face and hands was a whitish blue. There was no blood, no apparent marks of any kind that would indicate a cause of death. Prescott was quick to point that out to the others. "See! There are no wounds, nothing. It was a drowning, plain and simple."

With the cook and caretaker within earshot, the members eyed each other cautiously, wondering, waiting for someone to speak. No one dared to utter a word. Slowly, like the funeral yet to come, the Venture Club members followed the stretcher bearers in single file as the short procession wound its way up the hill. As the others moved on, Anders Johnson grabbed Arlo Peterson's arm, holding him back as the others continued toward the Camp.

"What is it?" Peterson spoke softly, aware that Johnson did not want the others to hear.

"Sally told me that Hannah is missing. Schmidt came and got her late last night, and she never came back."

Peterson, who was eyeing the others make their way slowly up the hill, turned and stared directly at Johnson. Though he said nothing, Johnson could tell that Peterson understood the two events were likely connected.

From the window of her room, Sally watched as the woeful parade wound its way up the hill, past the sleeping quarters, and on toward the lodge. She was not sure if it was remorse or anger that gnawed at her so vigorously as she watched the water-soaked body of Thomas Schmidt pass by. She made no attempt to hide from the men, but none looked in her direction. She did notice that two of them were hanging well back of the others, seemingly locked in a tense conversation.

"Peterson, it could be that the girl killed Schmidt," Johnson hypothesized. "God knows, he probably had it coming; you know how he could be. That would make sense, right? And after she did, she just lit out for Lax Lake to catch the cars back to Duluth."

To Peterson, it did make sense, and would provide a plausible and satisfactory solution to the problem. He might have wondered how a girl barely five feet tall and slight of build could overpower Schmidt, or how the body could have ended up in the lake. But those were details for another time. And even if it didn't happen exactly that way, it was a reasonable story; one they could hang on to, if needed. So for now, they would take the body to Lax Lake, wire the County Sheriff in Duluth, and bring this inconvenient incident to a close.

Chapter 13

In the dim light of the lodge, Stock now slid over to the corner of the great room and started rummaging through what appeared to be an old army footlocker. It was brown and battered, and carried a faint insignia of the United States Army. He soon emerged with a lever action rifle. It was Stock's pride and joy; a Winchester 1894 30-30 hunting rifle. He gave Andersen, who had crawled out of the kitchen, and was now lying beneath the pine table in the middle of the room, a quick wink. "Now we can fight back" Stock whispered confidently.

As Martin lay silently on the cold hard floor, a penetrating chill gripped him as the adrenaline began to fade from his bloodstream, and cold of the rough hewn floor seeped through his perspiration and blood stained wool shirt. Soon he was shivering uncontrollably; his teeth chattering so loud he was certain the shooter could hear him. As he lay there shaking, he could not decide if it was from the cold or from a suffocating fear of death.

Stock had now positioned himself in the far corner of the room, sitting with his back against the wall. Above him, one of the unlucky moose stared into the distance; appearing unconcerned about its unfortunate encounter with flying lead. Ben cradled the rifle in his arms like it was a newborn, looking more relaxed than he had any right to be. Finally, he interrupted the silence. "So your brother lured you into a death trap did he?" It was more a statement of fact than a question.

Martin made no reply. The possibility that it was his brother who had fired those shots struck him just a few minutes after the flying glass had left him shocked and bleeding in the kitchen. But was there another explanation? Possible, maybe, but Andersen was a man of science; a man who evaluated facts and information, whether in the operating room or in his life in the city. And it appeared the facts, as he knew them, could lead him to no other conclusion that his brother <u>had</u> lured him into a lethal trap.

Stock took notice of Martin's uncontrolled shivering, and with his rifle still tucked into the crook of his arm, grabbed the two fine wool blankets and pillow that Martin had laid so neatly near the hearth and pulled them over to the doctor. Andersen nodded, and gratefully shrouded himself in the blankets; soon curled up like a lazy pup beneath the pine table.

The dim glow of the exhausted fire was all that illuminated the room. Deep shadows obscured nearly every corner and feature of the lodge. It was clear to both them that they were now prisoners, certain that any attempt to leave the lodge would provoke a withering hail of bullets.

"He won't come for us tonight, Doc," Stock said casually. "I think he'll wait 'til morning."

Chapter 14

The gunshot was so loud and so close Hannah jumped from a mortal sleep to being fully awake in the wink of an eye. Cautiously she peeked out from her small fortress of balsam fir to see if her attacker had returned.

The previous night had been a horrific series of events that began when she heard Sally and the German, Mr. Schmidt, arguing in the front room of the women's sleeping quarters. Their voices were loud and agitated, though she could not make out what either was saying. Hannah and the other women had slipped away from the lodge several hours earlier when the men had become more interested in arguing and bragging to each other than anything the women had to offer.

Hannah Dahlgren, who was just 20, had joined the 'auxiliary' about a year ago. She was born and grew up in Taylor's Falls, Minnesota, one of four daughters born to Peter and Alice Dahlgren. Peter and Alice were proprietors of Dahlgren's Meat Market, a thriving butcher shop in the small but industrious town located on the St. Croix River. Well-respected by his fellow merchants and other prominent citizens, Peter had served as mayor for over 6 years.

From an early age, Hannah's beauty and sweet spirit were obvious to all who met her. She had shimmering blond hair, soft, well-proportioned features, and sparkling blue eyes that radiated innocence. She had a trim, shapely figure that grew buxom as she reached 'the bloom'. With a twinge of jealous sarcasm, her sisters referred to Hannah as the 'pretty one'. Behind her back, and occasionally to her face she was also known as the 'slow one'.

Though her parents put great emphasis on their children's education, book learning proved difficult for Hannah. She struggled with her lessons at school as well as those in life. At the age of 16, she believed that one of the boys who worked on the ferry that crossed the St. Croix River was in love with her, intent on taking Hannah as his wife. For the boy, it was nothing more than an exploration of his sexual appetites, and when a baby unexpectedly resulted from their union, he disappeared. Mayor Dahlgren was humiliated, and insisted that the baby be put up for adoption in another county. He also decided that Hannah must start a new life somewhere far from their small town near the falls.

Through a shirt-tail relation, Peter arranged for Hannah to become a nanny for one of the wealthy families that lived in the grand mansions that lined London Road in east Duluth. On a harsh winter's day in December, Peter Dahlgren discreetly dropped Hannah off at the train station in North Branch providing neither a hug, nor even a fatherly farewell.

For the next year or so, though treated as a servant, Hannah felt a sense of belonging to 'her' family. While mostly confined to the servants' quarters when not caring for the children, she worked with her typical naïve and caring spirit to watch over the children and tend her chores. She would often think of her own child, somehow knowing that she would never see the baby again.

After a time, the eldest son now 15, discovered his own sexual desires, and soon became enchanted by

Hannah's beauty. On a dark, early December's night with his parents in town he came calling. As icy, wind driven breakers crashed on the rocky shore of Lake Superior, he snuck into Hannah's tiny room and forced himself upon her. At first, Hannah resisted. But soon fearing that resistance would jeopardize her job, she acquiesced, letting him have his way.

Several weeks later, the boy, tortured by his actions, yet fearful of the real truth, revealed to his parents that he and the nanny had engaged in sexual relations; Hannah, he claimed, had forced herself on him.

After a noisy argument between the boy's parents, Hannah, with just her small carpet bag of meager belongings, was escorted from the mansion though the servants entrance, out into a harsh winter's morning on the cold streets of east Duluth.

These memories had come flooding back to Hannah as she heard the heated words echoing down the hall of the women's sleeping quarters. Then the voices went silent and suddenly Sally appeared holding a kerosene lamp in front of her. "Hannah," Sally hissed, "are you awake?" The light reflected off of Sally's red hair, giving her head an almost divine glow.

"Yes?" Hannah replied meekly.

"Mr. Schmidt wants you to walk with him."

"Now?"

Sally lowered the lamp to her waist, which caused eerie shadows to streak across her face. "Yes. He said it would be a short walk. He wants to clear his head, and wants to have a companion."

Hannah dressed hurriedly, draping a heavy wool shawl over her slender shoulders. Though the day had been warm, she knew the air cooled quickly when the sun disappeared behind the hills and forests to the west.

She entered the front room to find Schmidt standing, waiting. His eyes were blood-shot, and he swayed slightly from side to side. When he saw Hannah, he nodded his head impersonally and mumbled something she could not understand. As she moved closer to him, he spun on his heel and headed straight out the door. As he did, he stumbled, grabbing for the doorframe to steady himself. Never a gentleman, he flung the door open, and marched down the steps, expecting Hannah to follow him.

Once away from the log building, they walked through the cool, damp night, the sky filled with stars so bright they glistened like the leaded cut-glass crystals that dangle from expensive gas lamps. Schmidt, who was rarely talkative in any situation, said nothing as they walked slowly down the trail leading to Tettegouche Lake. As they approached the water's edge, the soft caress of lapping water on smooth rocks created a tranquil and soothing sound. For several long minutes he stood motionless, gazing across the placid waters, reflections of the stars twinkling on the surface of peaceful lake. Hannah shivered, pulling her thick shawl tightly around her while she waited quietly behind him.

Then, without warning, Schmidt spun around and struck her in the face with the back of his hand. She collapsed in a heap on the ground. He fell on top of her, grabbing her around the neck with one hand, while pulling up her long wool dress with the other. Hannah could not understand what was happening. She was familiar with Mr. Schmidt's rough and clumsy sexual advances, but this was different. There was fierceness and a viciousness that frightened Hannah more than she could imagine. Her survival instinct took control, willing her to fight back.

As Schmidt positioned himself on top of her, pulling her dress up to her waist, she yanked one of her knees upward with an adrenaline soaked thrust that was more powerful than she thought possible. As her knee buried itself deeply in Schmidt's groin he let out a nearly inhuman groan and cry, stunned by the searing pain in his testicles that reached all the way to his throat.

Frantically, Hannah clawed her way from Schmidt's reach, jumped to her feet and ran. With no clear destination in mind, she simply tried to put distance between her and her attacker. Stumbling over limbs and rocks, she fell several times, each time hopping quickly to her feet, while following the shoreline of the lake. Schmidt, after writhing in the mud for several minutes, nearly blinded by the excruciating pain, now staggered to his feet. He could not see the girl, but could hear her footsteps and snapping twigs coming from the shoreline.

"Come here you bitch," Schmidt screamed diabolically. "Hurt me, will you? Now you pay," as he moved slowly in the direction of the sounds. Each step sent lightning bolts of pain shooting from his groin into his belly. "Come here you God damned bitch, your nightmare is on its way."

Hannah was breathing heavily, and decided that she would try to hide. Standing on the edge of the lake, she could just barely make out what looked to be a small clump of balsam fir near the top of a rocky summit lying deep in the shadows.

As children, Hannah and her sisters would play 'hide and seek' in the steep hills above Taylor's Falls. She always found these clumps of small dense trees to be the best hiding places. So as she had done as a child when one of her sisters would start counting, she moved

71

quietly and carefully, trying to avoid making a sound that might give her away. Once she reached the thick copse of trees, she burrowed into the middle of them, wrapping herself protectively in her shawl while huddling silently on the carpet of soft, moist needles that blanketed the ground.

From the sound of his voice, it appeared that Schmidt was still following the shore of the lake, yelling for her to come 'meet her maker'. For a time, the voice trailed away as Schmidt moved further up the east shore nearly to the north side of the lake away from where Hannah was hiding. But then, his voice rounded back as Schmidt apparently began to retrace his steps coming in her direction.

Peeking cautiously out from her hiding spot, she caught a glimpse of Schmidt's silhouette against the starlit shimmer of the lake waters. He was hunched over, walking slowly and erratically, yelling curses into the dark night. Fortunately, he did not stray far from the lake as he continued to move back to where the attack took place.

Now, as he disappeared from her view, she heard a surprising noise. It was a sound that reminded her of when the young boys around Taylor's Falls would gather up the rotten pumpkins at the end of the season, and slap them with large wooden sticks. The seeds and soft pulp of the pumpkin would fly, as the stick made a hollow thud on the soft exterior of the pumpkin. Now that sound echoed across the lake, followed by a loud splash, and then, silence.

Hannah, unsure what had happened or what she should do curled up tightly in her shawl and lay silently among the fir. She closed her eyes, put her head down on the moist ground and quietly began to sob......

Now with the sun standing high overhead, a nearby gunshot had jolted her from her sleep. She cautiously peered out through the tree branches. There, standing down near the lake, the grey haired man, Mr. Peterson, was talking and pointing out into the water. A younger man, who looked to be Mr. Wentworth was standing nearby holding what appeared to be a large, shiny pistol. Hannah sat frozen, unable to move. Tears filled her eyes. Whatever had happened, she knew she was to blame.

Chapter 15

In the dark lodge, Stock sat quietly on the wood floor, slouched but alert, in the corner of the great room. His knees were pulled up to his chest, his rifle held tightly in both hands. "Doc, get some sleep, I'll take the first watch," he whispered.

Still lying under the table, his blankets wrapped as tightly around him as the burial linens of an Egyptian mummy, Martin felt his shivering began to subside. "You know, Ben, it might not be my brother out there. It could be someone else trying to kill us." Andersen's half-hearted attempt to pose an alternate explanation did little to convince either man.

"Well, maybe... maybe…a lot strange things happen out here." Stock replied with a comforting tone.

The fire was now a small mound of orange coals and ash and Stock felt like talking. Though he chose a life alone, he enjoyed conversation when given the chance. During his visits to Beaver Bay to sell furs and buy provisions he would make the rounds with the postmaster and store owners and others he knew growing up. He always marveled how things had changed in the last five years. But in some ways, the town and its people were very much the same. He was glad about that.

"Doc, where'd you get that pistol of your'n?" Stock inquired. "She's one powerful sidearm. I seen 'em blow a hole in a man the size of your fist." He clenched his fist and held it in front of his face for effect. Andersen was getting groggy as warmth and exhaustion wrapped around him as tightly as his blankets. He was puzzled by Sarge's question.

"One of my patients gave it to me," Martin murmured, keeping his eyes tightly closed. "He couldn't pay his bill and asked if I would take it in trade. He was in the war; suffered terribly from mustard gas. One of his lungs was so badly burned, I had to remove it."

"I was lucky," Stock responded wistfully, his head now tilted back against the log wall. "I wasn't in the trenches as much as some, mostly a supply sergeant. Those boys on the line.....they really got it....week after week of living in mud and disease, and then 'over the top'...so many boys killed. And for what....?" His voice trailed off as pain-soaked memories of life on the western front, still burning raw and horrific, came flooding back. Stock did not want to dwell on those memories and veered back to where he started. "Doc, I gotta say it don't make no sense to me that a body would hike all the way out here, looking for a brother they don't care nothin' about. Beside the letter, is there another reason you come?"

Andersen slowly exhaled. "Well Mr. Stock, I ..." He paused, considering whether he really wanted to, or simply needed to unburden himself of what lay so heavy on his mind. He opened his eyes widely, and began to reveal the circumstances that brought him to Tettegouche Camp.

"Our parents came to Duluth in 1895; immigrants from Sweden. There were four of us children, my two sisters, and my twin brother." Andersen was uncertain how much detail he should provide but the words now tumbled from his mouth like the cascades of an Arrowhead stream.

"Our parents took what little money they had and bought a small store located near the waterfront in east Duluth. Maybe you've seen it, Andersen Dry Goods Store on the corner of London Road and 15th Avenue?" Martin waited for some sort of response from Stock, but none was forthcoming. "Anyway, it became a thriving business selling to the rich families who were building the mansions along London Road."

Martin stopped. He had never shared with anyone, much less a complete stranger, what he was about to tell this man. Rolling over, he sat up with his back propped up against one of the table legs.

"Go on, Doc. What about that brother of your'n?" Stock urged.

"Well….in 1897, Matts contracted an especially virulent strain of influenza that was striking many in the city. He nearly died, and our mother claimed that it was one of God's miracles that Matts survived. I guess out of that fear and sense of near loss, Matts became the center of her universe and recipient of her unending devotion. And I became the 'other' twin." Realizing immediately, how shallow and petty that must sound, Martin felt like he needed to apologize.

Strangely, it now occurred to Stock, that Martin's journey into the wilderness may not be one of assistance; maybe it was one of revenge. Stock studied Martin's expression while he absently stroked his long red beard, which was streaked with tobacco juice. He was as confused as Martin by the events of the last hour. He had lived peacefully in this old, run down camp for several years now and very little ever happened to interfere with his hardscrabble routine; certainly nothing like this.

Before Martin could find the words, Stock launched another question. "So you come out here to kill him because of that?" Stock asked incredulously.

"No, no, no." Martin relied insistently, though the vigor of his response softened with each 'no'. "Ben, my brother is bad man. And I believe that he had something to do with the death of that railroad fellow here at the Camp and other crimes back in Duluth. So, to be honest, I am not sure why I came here; to help him, or to ......" his voice trailed off, leaving the sentence unfinished. Stock could tell there was a powder keg smoldering inside the good doctor.

Stock tried to sort through the confusion with a diversionary attack. "How did he get hooked up with those Venture Club fellas?"

"Do you know the Merritt family in Duluth?"

"Well, I sure know the name, but can't say I ever met any of 'em," Stock replied.

The Merritts were among the first settlers to put down stakes in the village of Duluth in the 1850's. With the discovery of iron ore in the Arrowhead in the 1870's, Leonidas Merritt and his four brothers and two cousins became known around the region as the Seven Iron Men, for their accomplishments in developing the highly productive iron mines in what became known as the Mesabi Iron Range.

"The Merritts were friends of my parents and for some reason Leonidas took a shine to Matts. I guess he felt sorry for him or something, and took him under his wing." With Merritt's influence, Matts went from office boy, to manager, and eventually to vice-president of the Mountain Iron Mine. It was his connections with Arlo Peterson that enabled Matts to become a member of the Venture Club.

"As I said, Mr. Stock, growing up, my mother adored Matts. He was the apple of her eye." Martin stopped as tears began to pool in his eyes. "She never really had much time for me. I was a good son, supported my parents and worked hard for everything I have. She never noticed or even seemed to care. It was always Matts who received her love and attention. I think I grew to resent her for that." Martin paused as he felt a teardrop slowly trickle down the bridge of his nose.

"Well she died about a month ago after suffering so from the cancer. During her time in the hospital, Matts never came to see her. Not once. Yet, despite all her suffering and longing for him to come, all she could do was make excuses for him, saying he would come if he could. He never did."

Suddenly, the hasp on the main lodge door began to rattle. Someone was trying to come in. In the faint light Martin could see the drop latch slowly rise. Fortunately, the deadbolt and brace secured the door tightly as someone or something slowly leaned against it.

Stock reacted without uttering a word. He snapped the rifle to his shoulder, and a fountain of orange fire erupted from the end of the gun's barrel, briefly illuminating the room as he shot straight through the door. The explosion of a 30-30 shell contained within the walls of the lodge was deafening. Without hesitation, he cocked the lever, chambering another cartridge. As Martin yelled, "Nooooo! " a second blast of orange fire and ear-shattering noise shook the windows as the stench of spent gunpowder filled the room. And then… nothing…. but silence.

With just a hint of sarcasm, Stock whispered, "guess I was wrong 'bout him waiting til mornin'." Lying under the table, wrapped tightly in his woolen cocoon, Martin again began to shake violently.

Chapter 16

Hannah watched as the man with the pistol ran up the hill. She continued to watch as the others returned. Intently, she watched as they fished a body out of the lake; she couldn't be positive, but she was pretty sure it was Mr. Schmidt. It had to be. That explained the splashing noises she heard last night. She watched as they carried the body up the hill and disappeared from sight over the top of the rise. She remained motionless among the fir trees, consumed with the burning fear that she had killed a man, and would be going to jail or maybe even hanged.

As the group assembled back at the lodge, Peterson instructed the hired men to place the stretcher in one of the wagons, and hook up a pair of horses. While they did, the remaining Venture Club members entered the lodge to work out their story. "We'll do as the lawyer suggested," Peterson said firmly. "Me and the hired man will take the body to town. From there, I'll send a telegraph to the Sheriff's Office telling him that we had an unfortunate accident here at the camp, and poor Mr. Schmidt has died. We'll put his body on the first train heading south. I can arrange with a mortician I know in Duluth to pick up the body and prepare it for burial. Who is the county sheriff in this county?"

"We're in Lake County, but they don't have a sheriff, so the law is handled by St. Louis County,"

Wentworth answered knowingly. "We need to alert the County Sheriff in Duluth."

"Willis Chambers?" Peterson replied with a tone that was part question and part relief.

"Yes, that's right," Wentworth replied. "Do you know him?"

A crooked smile creased Peterson's face. "Oh yes, we go back a few years. Matter of fact, I was the one who convinced him to run for sheriff, and maybe even helped him get elected."

"So he will believe you when you tell him that this was an accident," Prescott interjected with growing confidence that the situation would now be handled in the right way.

Billy O'Leary and Anders Johnson were not so quick to jump on board the speeding train that was heading, in their view, away from the truth. "I'm still thinking that Scottie had something to do with this sad affair, and we need to figure that out 'fore we go telling everybody a pack a lies," O'Leary stated firmly as he stared directly at Alan Prescott.

Johnson, who was standing slightly to the left and behind O'Leary, nodded his head vigorously as Billy spoke. Prescott glared at O'Leary and took a threatening step in his direction. "If you got some proof you goddamn mick, you better show it now," he growled as his face turned a beet red, his fists tightly clenched. Peterson knew from experience that O'Leary was not a man to back away from a fight, so he slid between the two men, trying to insure reason and order.

As Peterson attempted to calm the mood, Wentworth, for some odd reason, began to notice the uncomfortable weight of his Colt revolver. Slowly, he unbuckled the gun belt and placed the leather and steel in a pile on the large pine table. "One thing Arlo," said

Wentworth seemingly quoting statutes from memory, "the law requires that if there is any question whatsoever, about the cause of death, an autopsy must be conducted by the county coroner."

Surprised by this new information, Scottie glanced at Peterson. "Who is the coroner. Do you know him?" Peterson shook his head, and for a moment there was silence. Then Matts Andersen, who had not uttered a word throughout the morning's ordeal, cleared his throat, drawing all eyes in his direction.

"The county coroner is my brother, my twin brother, Martin Andersen."

A wry smile returned to Prescott's face.

Chapter 17

S ally stepped out into the bright sunlight and walked purposefully toward Einar and Ben who were hitching up a muscular pair of Morgan horses to one of the wagons. "Where are you going?" she demanded fiercely as the two men busily outfitted the chestnut stallions with horse collars and traces.

"I guess we're tak'n Mr. Schmidt's body into Lax Lake," Ben replied while cinching up the thick leathers harnesses and looping the reins back to the wagon.

"Isn't anyone going to look for Hannah?"

Einar leaned in toward Ben and whispered in Finnish, "Mika han aikoa?"

"Hannah is missing, she's 'puuttuva'," Ben answered slowly and distinctly. Einar looked confused, and nodded slowly, as a sad expression swept over his face. It was clear to Sally that these men were in no position to make a decision like that, so she headed toward the lodge to confront the Venture Club members.

The men had just finished their conversation, and were silently filing out of the lodge; Arlo Peterson in the lead. Looking up, he saw Sally approaching and quickly recognized from the dark look on her face, that her Irish was up and nothing good was about to happen.

"When are you <u>men</u> going to look for Hannah?" she said, nearly spitting the word 'men' in Peterson's face. As she did, she lifted her left arm, and pointed out into the vast wilderness.

"Sally we've got a situation here. We need to get Schmidt's body into Lax Lake, and down to Duluth." Peterson's tone was equally sharp. He was unaccustomed to anyone, much less a whore, talking to him like that.

"Well, it doesn't take half a dozen men to haul a dead body into town," Sally shot back.

Peterson stopped and turned. Though he considered it a fool's errand to look for someone who had likely hightailed it to town many hours ago, he wanted to keep the situation in his control and knew Sally would not go away quietly.

"Wentworth and O'Leary, you two go with Sally and help her look for the girl." Surprised but compliant, the men glanced at each other, and then nodded in Peterson's direction. The mid afternoon sun was now bright and warm. The fresh breeze was laced with the sweet smell of dogwood blossoms. It was a most pleasant day to pursue such an unpleasant task. Wentworth and O'Leary followed closely in Sally's wake as she steamed down the trail toward the lake.

Since their acquaintance several years ago, Billy had developed an odd kinship and a full ration of respect for Sally; in part due to their shared Irish heritages, but mostly for his appreciation of her determined spunk and courage. Though he too believed they were wasting their time looking for someone who did not want to be found, he was willing to go along, if only for Sally's benefit.

Standing at the water's edge, she bent close to the ground, pointing out several small, sharp heeled footprints that lay among larger, flat soled prints in the muddy patches scattered among the rocks.

"Hannah was here," Sally announced loudly. "Look at these footprints!"

Now, with their eyes drawn to the muddy impressions, Wentworth and O'Leary began to follow the trail of tracks that seemed to head north along the eastern shore of the lake. Intermittent eruptions of bedrock, and random collections of glacier strewn stone, made it difficult to follow the trail, but with enough low spots to aid them, they kept moving. Then, on a deadfall, John Wentworth found a bit of cloth snagged up by a sharp tree branch. Checking it carefully, Sally pronounced, "I am sure that this came from the dress Hannah was wearing last night."

About half way up the east shore, the smaller footprints seemed to disappear, while the larger, flat soled prints continued on. The men pressed forward following those prints as Sally stood transfixed at the spot where the last of the smaller prints ended. Gazing up the hill from the lake, Sally saw what appeared to be another fragment of Hannah's ankle length dress caught in a prickly bush part way up the hill.

Clamoring up the steep incline, she retrieved the shred of cloth, which matched the first. Further up the slope, Sally noticed a small clump of balsam fir near the crest of the hill. A feeling of intuition came over her, which settled into the pit of her stomach. As the men continued to scour the shoreline further north, Sally made her way toward the patch of trees. As she approached, she heard soft whimpers coming from deep inside the dark green den. Reaching out her arm, Sally swept aside several of the small trees to reveal Hannah sitting cross-legged on the ground, her shawl pulling tightly around her, and streams of tears rolling down her cheeks.

"Oh, Sally," Hannah wailed collapsing into the fir needles. "I killed Mr. Schmidt."

Chapter 18

Even before the first faint traces of morning light began to filter through the upper windows of the lodge, Stock and Andersen were wide awake. Stock had slept little during the night, dosing lightly for a few minutes at a time.

For Martin, the fearful events of the past evening had been swallowed up by bone-weary exhaustion. He had drifted off into a deep, if fitful sleep; sometimes snoring, occasionally talking out loud. At times, during the endless night, Stock wondered if Martin was talking to him. But most of the words were mumbled and indecipherable. The only phrase that Stock could clearly understand was "never again" which Andersen had muttered several times. Now, as the lodge began to brighten, both men were awake; hungry, cold, and anxious.

"Martin?" Stock hissed.

"Yes?"

"Ya hungry?"

"Starving."

"I got dried trout and venison here in my larder," Stock reported, "and canned salmon in the kitchen."

To a man as hungry as Martin, most any food sounded good. However, a trip into the kitchen might expose them to more gunfire. "The trout or venison sounds fine," Martin replied. Stock opened the top of a sturdy hand-hewn cedar box about 2 feet square that was tucked into the corner of the lodge. Out came two thick strips, each about a foot long, of clay red meat that was stiff and dry. Though tough and chewy, Martin found the dry smoked venison tasty and satisfying. While they chewed like a pair of dairy cows until their jaws ached, they both wished for some water to help wash down their breakfast, no matter how rusty it might taste.

"Well Doc, I got a plan."

Andersen, still lying on his back tightly swaddled in his blankets, stopped chewing for a moment. He was suddenly embarrassed, realizing that he had given no thought at all to how they may escape their log prison.

Ben, on the other hand, had spent most of night grinding through options and ideas, and was now ready to move forward with vengeance. He felt like a caged animal. For the last four years, he had gone where he wanted, when he wanted, without thought or constraint. Now he was being controlled by someone else, and it was a feeling that he could not, would not tolerate any longer. He looked over at Martin, huddled under the table, likely filled with fear and doubt. Fortunately for them, fear and doubt were two traits that Benjamin Stock had in very short supply. He laid out his plan to Martin

First, if they were real lucky, one or both of his shots through the door the previous night had already ended the drama, and they might find Martin's brother lying in a heap outside the door. That was possible, Stock imagined, but not something they could count on. He might have nicked him, bloodied him, and the man may have decided to leave the area while he was still able to do so. Again, nothing they could count on.

"Doc, here's what I'm thinkin'. Your brother can't cover both sides of the lodge at the same time. So, we attack on two fronts. We tip that big old table over on its side and put in front of the main door. You get behind it with that hand cannon of your'n and I'll throw open the door."

Martin's head was spinning as he tried to comprehend the audacity and risks that Stock was suggesting. Yet Ben appeared implausibly confident as his voice began to rise with excitement.

"What happens if he starts shooting at me?" Martin asked meekly.

"Perfect," Stock blurted out; his blood now up. "Then we know he's covering that door. While you fire off a barrage from your Colt to pin him down, I'll slip out the back door and flank him." Stock was certain that his knowledge of the area, and his experience as a soldier and hunter would give him a sizable advantage once he got into the woods.

"What happens if the man is not on this side?" While Stock plan seemed simple enough, Martin could imagine all kinds of problems; most of which led to one or both of them ending up dead.

"Then I make break for the woods through this door, and get the drop on him when he comes around from the other side. Doc, here we ain't nothin' but fish in a barrel, and that's gotta change," Stock said soberly. "This fish is gonna jump up and bite 'em," he added with defiance.

Andersen grabbed his backpack, and carefully removed the M1911 from its soft white cloth wrappings. Digging around in the bag, he located four fully loaded, 12 round magazines that had sifted to the bottom of the bag during his trek to the Camp. Gathering them up, he set them with painstaking care on the pine table, realizing that he would now have to make an admission that would put Ben's plan in jeopardy.

"Mr. Stock," Martin began haltingly, before clearing his throat. "I have never fired this gun before, never even loaded it....and.... to tell you.... the truth, I have never fired a gun of any kind it my life." Andersen bowed his head; now ashamed of something that, until this moment, he had never considered shameful.

Stock gave him a long sideways glance. This fellow really was a cake-eater, he thought to himself. Then with a slight shake of the head, he let out a hearty belly laugh. "Well, Doc, you picked one hell of time to learn." Sarge grabbed the handgun, and expertly demonstrated how the magazine slid neatly into the handle. He demonstrated how to eject the magazine, and insert a new one. He showed Martin where the safety was located, and how it clicked on and off. When he was finished, he pulled back the slide which chambered a cartridge and cocked the hammer. Clicking the safety on, he handed it back to Andersen.

"You're cocked and loaded, Doc. Once you're ready, slip off the safety and let her fly."

Andersen held the heavy pistol gingerly as he would sometimes grasp a new scalpel, trying to become familiar with its weight and balance. But this was not a scalpel, and the size and weight of the fearsome weapon scared him to death.

Together, Stock and Andersen flipped the heavy pine table on its side in front of the doorway, just far enough away to allow the door to swing fully open. Martin, pistol in hand, positioned himself behind the heavy table placing the handle of the gun on its side rail to steady his aim. He crouched on the floor so that just his eyes and the top of his head peeked above the table. The barrel of the pistol wavered wildly, despite Martin's attempts to control his nervous twitching. In a moment of regret, he wondered why he was still not lying underneath this table wrapped tightly in his warm blankets instead of crouching behind it clutching a cold, deadly weapon.

Stock offered some last minute instructions. "Wrap both hands around the handle, Doc. That gun'ill rip your arm off, if you're not ready for it. Brace yourself, and keep squeezing the trigger, slowly and surely until she's out of cartridges. Once I'm out the door, close and brace this one, then get to the back door as fast as you can and do the same."

Martin tried to digest and burn Stock's instructions into his memory, but he was mostly fixated on the cold hunk of steel in his right hand. Giving the doctor a warm look of confidence, Stock grabbed his rifle, levered a cartridge into the chamber, and readied himself near the door. Slowly he slid the door brace from its brackets, setting it quietly on the floor. Then with a sly smile and quick nod, he jerked open the latch, and yanked firmly on the door handle. It swung open with a rusty groan, as Stock flattened himself against the log wall.

The outdoors now appeared before Martin, like the parting of stage curtain. His heart began to pound wildly and breathes came in short puffs. With an odd mixture of relief and disappointment he saw no body, nor any sign of blood on the front step. Slowly, he began to rise from his crouch, straining to see anything that might provide evidence that their nightmare was over. The unexpected wiggle of leaves and branches caused by a frisky red squirrel leaping from one tree to the next forced him back behind the table.

He stole a quick glance in Stock's direction, still plastered against the wall. The morning light was sufficient to see well into the forest. The energetic singing of several songbirds and the gentle rush of a placid morning breeze were the only sounds.

Twack, blam…. The sickening sound of a lead slug burying itself in the pine table followed immediately by the explosion of the gunpowder that had propelled it shattered the silence. Martin fell to his knees, seeking shelter behind the table, and suddenly wondering whether the table was thick enough to stop a hurtling hunk of lead.

"Now's the time to learn how to shoot Doc," Stock yelled. Martin collected himself, steadied the gun on the edge of the table, and squeezed the trigger. It roared with an ear shattering blast. The vigor of the recoil all but ripped the gun from his hands, forcing his arms nearly backward behind his head. Willing himself to overcome the startling energy of exploding gunpowder, he forced his arms back down and squeezed the trigger again, and again, and again. He didn't aim at anything in particular, but spread the barrage across his field of vision through the open door. Apparently the ferocity of the .45 semi-automatic momentarily silenced the attacker as no shots were returned in his direction.

As soon as Martin had squeezed off the second shot, Sarge was sprinting toward the back door, staying out of the sightline of the open entry. As he ran, he kept a mental tally of the number of shots that Andersen fired. By the fifth shot, he had removed the door brace and was out the back door, closing it tightly behind him. He counted shots 8, 9, and 10 as he made his way away from the building and well into the woods. By the time he heard number 12, he was around the south side of the lodge, 70 yards deep in the woods. Lying on his stomach, clutching his gun tightly to his body, he heard the sound of the lodge door slamming shut. Martin was, or so Ben hoped, locked safely inside.

"Now the hunted, becomes the hunter," Stock whispered softly to himself.

Chapter 19

Sally glanced over her shoulder, trying to locate
Wentworth and O'Leary. Through the dense
mantle of bright green leaves, she could see that
the men had now wandered well up the east shore of
Tettegouche Lake, nearly to the north end. Their
muffled voices echoed softly across the water as they
talked, but Sally could not make out what they were
saying. Turning back toward Hannah, her mind raced as
she tried to piece together what had happened the night
before. Was it possible that Hannah had actually killed
Mr. Schmidt? That seemed very unlikely, but was it
possible? Maybe he was so drunk; it didn't take much to
push him into the water…and nature did the rest.

"Hannah, be quick and tell me what happened,"
Sally whispered urgently as she again glanced over her
shoulder. She knew the men would soon return, and
imagined they would be quite pleased to find a
convenient scapegoat for the crime, if indeed one had
been committed.

Child-like Hannah wiped her eyes and nose with
her shawl. No longer a radiant young woman, she was
now a sad little girl. "Sally, Mr. Schmidt hit me, and
tried to, well, ah… you know. But he was so rough and
so mean, I just couldn't, you know." A stream of tears
trickled down Hannah's cheeks as she spoke between
pained sobs. "When he wouldn't stop, I kneed
him…..you know…..and then I ran off."

Sally could now imagine the events of the previous night. In the darkened woods, a vulgar man filled with anger and frustration attacks a simple young girl, who once again in her cheerless life was victimized by a merciless man. "Hannah we need to get you out of here," Sally said firmly. "But first I need to make sure those men don't find you."

She instructed Hannah to stay hidden in the fir trees as Sally bounded back down the hill toward the lake. Wentworth and O'Leary were now retracing their steps, still chatting between themselves. Seeing Sally nearly flying down the hill, O'Leary called to her. "Sally girl, what have you been doing up there?"

"A ladies' necessary, if you must know," Sally replied tartly. For her and others like her, lying to men was a necessary art and a well-honed skill. With practiced ease, she began to spin a story, certain the two men would accept it without question. "I found another scrap of Hannah's dress up the hill, and more of her footprints. I'm all but certain that she did head for Lax Lake. She's probably already there, or maybe even on the train to Duluth. She is surely long gone from this place by now."

Sally sounded convincing, and the two men were tired of looking. If she was willing to give up the search, they were more than happy to oblige. Together, they made their way back to the camp to report their findings to Peterson. As they approached, they could see that the wagon was now loaded, and two horses were eager to lean into their harnesses. Arlo was sitting on the wagon's bench seat next to the caretaker giving some last minute instructions to the Venture Club members who would remain behind.

93

"I'll be back as soon as I can," he announced loudly. "Ben, here will go with me. You make sure the other women stay in their quarters." He stopped abruptly as he noticed O'Leary, Johnson, and Sally approaching. Yelling out to them, he asked, "Well, what did you find?"

Moving close to the wagon, Sally shaded her eyes with her hand as she looked directly up at Peterson. Speaking with solemn conviction, she replied, "Looks like you were right Mr. Peterson. It appears Hannah has taken out for town."

O'Leary was quick to support Sally's version of the story. "Yes, appears she is already back in town, and probably in Duluth. We found some tracks that led in that direction." Peterson and the others felt a sense of relief. If the accidental death theory didn't pass muster, they now had a convenient scapegoat.

With a snap of the reins, and several clicks of his tongue, Ben urged the horses forward. Within a few minutes, the wagon disappeared behind a wall of trees, though the creaking of wood and leather and clopping of iron hooves on bare rock could be heard for several more minutes as the men and their cargo made their way toward Lax Lake. Once out of sight, Sally hitched up her long dress, and moved quickly in the direction of the women's sleeping quarters. "Where you going Sally, girl?" O'Leary called to her.

"I need some rest," she said in a tone dripping with distain. She did not even bother to look back. Once she had disappeared up the rough wooden steps and into the building, the men milled about aimlessly. They were not really sure what to do. Over time, they had gotten comfortable with Arlo Peterson making decisions and setting the agenda for their group. Now, as the sound of his wagon slowly faded in the distance, they were on their own. After several minutes, Wentworth finally spoke up. "I don't know about you men, but after all that's happened today, I need a stiff drink."

The others nodded compliantly as Prescott turned toward Einar Toivenen and spoke with a nasty callousness few men could, or would ever care to replicate. "Make us something to eat."

Einar, feeling confused and lost without Ben nearby, nodded submissively. As he headed into the lodge, he was followed by the Venture Club members; all except John Wentworth and Matts Andersen, who hung back, leaning against a tight clump of paper birch that stood half-way between lodge and stable. Johnson noticed that they were not joining the rest. "You two coming?"

Wentworth answered first. "I'll be right there."

Andersen, his face now ashen and downcast replied, "No, I'm tired, I'm going to lie down for a while." With that, he turned and headed toward the men's bunk house. Johnson shrugged and followed the others into the lodge as the smell of wood smoke from the cast iron stove began to sweeten the afternoon air.

Chapter 20

After slamming the front door closed, and replacing the brace, Andersen ran toward the side exit. In a few anxious seconds he was able to replace the brace on that door as well. Now, thinking clearly he returned to his table fortress, locating one of the magazines he had laid there with such care. Though his hands were still shaking wildly, he was able to eject the empty magazine from the pistol. However, the barrel of the gun was so hot that he burned his hand as he clumsily attempted to slide the fresh magazine into the handle. Swearing to himself, he finally heard the comforting click of the ammunition clip as it locked into place. Carefully grabbing the slide as Stock had shown him, he cocked the pistol.

He now looked around the lodge, which had brightened considerably as the sun began to creep higher in the sky. Where should he position himself? How could he cover both entrances? For God's sake, what was happening outside?

Deep in the woods, Stock lay quietly on a damp blanket of leaves. Straining his eyes and ears, he attempted to locate their attacker. He had seen no movement, heard no sound since settling into his hiding spot among a thick patch of aspen and birch trees. Now it was a waiting game; his waiting game.

As an experienced deer hunter, he had learned to stalk game slowly, listening for telltale sounds, or any flash of movement that told him that his prey was near. White tail deer, with their superior hearing and eyesight were difficult for any hunter to ambush. But over the years, Stock had honed his already keen senses, exhibiting great patience and skill as he waited for his quarry to make the first move.

Slowly and silently, he edged forward to gain a more favorable position to observe the area in front of the lodge. Inhaling and expelling the cool morning air in slow, metered breaths, he remained motionless; only his eyes darted back and forth as he studied the landscape.

As the minutes ticked by, Stock began to consider the possibility that the man had made a run for it when Martin opened up with his hand gun. Stock had seen experienced soldiers take flight when the .45 caliber spoke; it could be that Martin's brother had decided that this fight had turned into something much more than he had bargained for. More time went by, and still no movement or sound; except for the raucous calls of several assertive blue jays re-establishing their territory, and the dull rhythmic thud of a hungry woodpecker pounding its way through a rotting tree trunk in search of grubs.

More minutes passed, and then he saw it. There among a thick tangle of raspberry bushes maybe 50 yards directly in front of the lodge entrance he caught a glint of reflected sunlight. Probably from the barrel of the gun that had haunted them the previous night, he guessed. Then, a minute later, he saw another bit of reflected sunlight. Stock began to sort his options. He could make a direct attack. After opening up with a well-placed salvo from his 30-30, he could go over the top and take his enemy straight on. Or he could execute a flanking maneuver; circling around to his left, using the trees and a slight rise in the landscape, to shield him from the attacker's view, from where he could sneak in from behind. He decided to take the indirect approach.

Carefully wriggling though the underbrush he distanced himself from the front of the lodge. Then getting to his feet, he hunched over, and began to pick his way around to the far side of the rise. After making his way several hundred yards deeper into the woods, he made a broad circle back toward the lodge. As he reached the top of the rise that lay between Nipisquit Lake and the lodge, he fell on all fours, sneaking silently toward the raspberry bushes.

Reminding himself to be patient, Stock stopped and lay silently for several minutes, straining to detect any sound or movement. In the distance, the front of the lodge was bathed in brilliant morning sunlight streaming in from behind, over Stock's shoulder. Stock smiled as he realized that he would be employing the same tactic that had provided a sizeable advantage to the flying aces in the Great War; falling upon their enemy directly out of the sun, blinding their foe to their impending demise.

Suddenly, inexplicably, the front door of the lodge was thrown open, and standing in the doorway, with his arms raised, waving some sort of white rag was Doc Andersen. 'My God, what the hell is he doing,' Stock whispered to himself.

Instinctively and protectively, Stock jumped to his feet and leveled his Winchester toward the area around the raspberry bushes. At the first sign of movement, he was prepared to empty the magazine of his trusty rifle, and end this fight. But no motion was detected. As Andersen continued to stand in the doorway, waving his flag, Stock made his way down the slope toward the bushes, the gun at his shoulder, his finger on the trigger.

Then, from nowhere a shot rang out and Stock felt a burning sensation under his left arm. He dropped to the ground as another shot whistled just over his head. Where were the shots coming from? Obviously, his prey was not hiding in the raspberry bushes after all.

Examining his wound, he saw that the bullet had sliced between his arm and chest, just below his armpit. The damage would have been slight except the bullet furrowed inside his bicep and nicked the brachial artery on the inside of Stock's arm. Blood now squirted from the wound with each beat of this heart. From his time on the western front, he knew that if this type of blood loss was not stopped quickly, he would soon pass out, and then, pass on.

Lying flat on his back, he stripped off his leather belt and with one hand cinched it as tightly as he could around his upper arm above the wound. The blood flow diminished substantially, but he knew the tourniquet was just a temporary fix. Without help, his prospects of survival were grim.

As he laid there, considering his next move, much to his amazement, the front door of the lodge, which had slammed shut when the shots rang out, slowly swung open and the M1911 came back into the fight.

Like before, slowly yet forcefully, Andersen was laying down a covering barrage. But this time it was focused on one spot, an area far to south of the lodge. Stock knew he had one chance to survive and that was to make a run for it.

Grabbing his rifle, he scrambled to his feet, and began running; frantically zigging and zagging through the brush, bent deeply at the waist, staying as low as possible. He charged through the brush and trees nearly out of control, propelled by pure adrenaline and the downward slope of the hill. Stock knew it was a do or die race to the safety of the lodge.

Again, he kept track of the number of shots fired as he ran; like a man possessed by the devil. At the 10th shot, he was nearly to the door. Only then did the attacker return fire, burying two quick shots in the side of the lodge near the doorway. Out of control, and at a speed faster than he thought possible, Stock crashed into and over the large pine table, nearly flattening Martin in the process. With his last bullet expended, and Ben lying safely in a heap on the cold wooden floor, Andersen slammed the door and jammed home the brace.

Breathing heavily, the sleeve of his jacket soaked in blood, Stock looked up into the terrified eyes of the doctor and said stoically, "Well, that didn't go so good."

Chapter 21

S ally peered cautiously from her window, watching as the men entered the lodge. She suspected they would remain there, eating and drinking until Mr. Peterson returned. During her time as a member of the auxiliary it was clear that Mr. Peterson was the leader of the group; little happened without him starting it or allowing it.

Without a word to the other women, who had not ventured from their rooms, Sally headed out the door and back into the woods. Over the last hour, gauzy high thin clouds had begun sliding across the sky, from the southwest. Now, they were followed by chunkier, darker, more forbidding ones. The sun, which had been so warm and bright earlier in the day, was now just a summer memory as the sky darkened.

Sally knew she had little time to improvise Hannah's escape. She was certain that if the men asked the frightened girl directly, she would, as she told Sally, tell them that she had killed Mr. Schmidt. For Hannah's sake, it was essential that conversation never take place. Moving swiftly, she made her way down the steep trail. Once she reached the lake, Sally wound her way up the shore line until she located the spot where Hannah's footprints had headed up the hill. From there she began to scale the rocky incline, until she spotted the clump of fir trees where Hannah had hidden herself the night before. Approaching, slowly and quietly, Sally whispered Hannah's name when she was near enough to be heard. "Hannah, its Sally. I have come for you. Are you alright?"

For several seconds there was nothing but the sound of the wind whistling through the tree tops, suddenly whipping them into a frenzy. Then she heard the soft whimpering of the young girl, who still believed that she was a murderer. "I'm here, Sally. I'm so glad you came back for me. I don't know what I would have done, if you hadn't."

Standing now for the first time in many hours, Hannah was as wobbly as a newborn colt as she stepped out from among the fir trees. Her eyes were swollen and bloodshot, and her radiant blond hair was a tangled mess, liberally sprinkled with fir needles, soggy brown leaves and bits of twigs. Sally couldn't help but offer a sad smile while feeling overwhelmed by pangs of sorrow for the poor girl. Now embracing her, Hannah felt as stiff and cold as a human being could, while remaining on this side of the river Styx. For some time, they held each other, finding relief and comfort from each other's warm embrace and simple presence. Finally, Sally stepped back, and firmly placed her hands on Hannah's shoulders while staring deeply into her eyes.

"We need to get you out of here." Sally said firmly. "Not just here, but out of this area. I have a good friend who works for Cadwallader Washburn at the flour mill in Minneapolis. He has helped me find work for other girls who wanted to….needed to start over, to start a new life. I know he would help you get a job there."

Staring back at Sally, Hannah's face suddenly took on a mask of shocked disbelief. For just that moment, Sally tried to understand how her suggestion could cause such a dramatic reaction from the girl. But what Sally could not know was that standing directly behind her was a man clutching a long wooden club which he, without hesitation, brought crashing down on Sally's skull, as Hannah stood paralyzed in fear.

The heavy club made a hollow sound as it collided with the top of Sally's head and she collapsed in a heap on the soft blanket of leaves. To Hannah's surprise, it was the same sound she had heard the previous night when Mr. Schmidt died.

Chapter 22

Martin stared down at the dirty, bloody lump of Benjamin Stock lying on his back. A leather belt was cinched tightly around his upper arm; his left hand was the color of ripe blueberries, a deep blue, nearly purple, a sure sign that the leather tourniquet, though likely keeping him alive was now jeopardizing his left arm below the elbow. With no blood flow to feed and nourish the cells and tissues, they would soon die, turning his skin to a gangrenous black.

Without a word to his patient, Doctor Andersen located his first aid kit, which contained a small scalpel, needle and sutures. The large pine table that had so ably served as his fortress would now become his operating table. Taking every ounce of his strength, Martin was able to flip the table upright as Stock looked on quizzically.

Whether due to his substantial loss of blood, or maybe because Stock was being Stock, the former caretaker asked with great earnestness, "Is it time for supper?"

"Ben, can you stand up?" Andersen asked. Not waiting for a reply, the question now became a threatening command. "Stand up. Get on the table. Now!"

With Martin's help, Stock was able to wobble to his feet just long enough to collapse on the table. Again, flat on his back, he looked straight up toward the peak of the great room, which began to slowly spin around him. The outline of the log rafters became blurry and he felt as if he were floating on a small wooden raft; tossing and bobbing as he fought to hang on. Then he heard someone yelling his name.

"Ben.... Ben.... lower the sail. Can't hold 'er in this wind."

Ben turned and faced the stern of their weathered fishing boat which was far out in the deep cold emptiness of Lake Superior. Pap was at the tiller, frantically trying to steer the tiny craft between rollers that were growing larger and more menacing by the minute. Ben snatched up the halyards that were whipping wildly across the deck, and began hauling on the cold, slippery ropes trying to lower the violently flapping mainsail.

As the small boat pitched uncontrollably in the heavy seas, Pap yelled again over the crashing waves. Ben could not make out what he was saying."What?"he screamed with all the voice he could muster.

"The girl, she's at the bottom of the lake, you know."

Stock, his hands now raw from clinging tightly to the ropes, couldn't believe or couldn't comprehend what his father was saying. "What?" he yelled again, just as a large wave broke over the bow of the boat, soaking him to the bone with icy water.........

As Stock lost consciousness, Martin knew he was racing the clock. With the severe loss of blood he had suffered, his vital organs would soon start shutting down. As one of just three surgeons in northeastern Minnesota, Dr. Martin Andersen was well practiced in dealing with all forms of injury; from industrial accidents, where men would arrive with their bodies crushed or limbs broken or missing. Others came in bleeding heavily from wicked knife wounds acquired at the local saloon.

Taking a pair of heavy scissors from his kit, he cut Stock's buckskin jacket and putrid wool shirt from around his bloody arm. He knew the tourniquet must stay in place, or it would be nearly impossible to suture up the hole in his brachial artery. Once the arm was free, he liberally soaked the wound with alcohol as blood continued to drip at a steady and alarming rate, pooling on the pine table, before eventually dripping onto the floor. Despite the primitive conditions and dim light, Martin was able to cut back the skin to expose the damaged artery. In minutes, he neatly stitched together the small furrow in the blood vessel. Then using the same suture thread, he pulled the edges of the skin tightly together over the wound. 'Not my best work', Martin thought to himself. However, he doubted Ben would be too concerned by the angry scar he would carry the rest of his life; however long that might be.

As soon as Martin finished closing the wound, he slowly released the tourniquet from Stock's arm. As he did, he studied the stitches for signs of leakage. He was pleased to see that only a few drops of blood oozed from his handiwork. He now turned his attention to Stock's forearm and hand. Thankfully, within several minutes, the purple began to fade to blue, then red, and finally a more normal skin color, as oxygen rich blood reached the veins of his extremity. Finishing his work, he wrapped and tied a large gauze bandage around his arm.

As the icy water dripped from Stock's face, he stared back at his father. But now sitting in his place calmly holding the tiller as the wind blew through her long blond hair, was a girl, THE girl, the one who ran off after the German was found drowned. He remembered her now....

With that, he awoke with a start, bathed in cold sweat. The room that had been so bright and sunny had now turned grey and shadowy. It took him several seconds to recall where he was and how he got there. His first sensation was that his left arm hurt like hell. Then he recalled Pap's haunting voice, and the girl, who looked so young, but seemed so calm steering their tiny boat through the frenzied whirlwind.

"Ben.... Sarge, how are you feeling?"

Stock slowly turned his head, and saw the doctor sitting in Stock's pressback chair slowly rocking back and forth, his face portraying a look of fear and apprehension. In his lap was the pistol that he held tightly in his right hand. On the floor, next to him, was Stock's rifle.

"My arm hurts like a son of a bitch. Whadda do to me?"

Martin lifted himself up from the chair and approached his patient. Though Ben's face was still white and pasty, a bit of color was returning to his cheeks. But his lips were dry and cracked. "Here Sarge, drink this. With as much blood as you lost, we need to get liquid into you as fast as possible." Andersen propped up Stock's head, and held a large tin cup to Ben's lips so he could drink deeply. Stock believed it was the best water he had ever tasted. After several more deep gulps, he began to feel his mind and body

107

start to float back together. He attempted to sit up, but Andersen forcefully placed his hand on Stock's chest. "Don't," he warned firmly. "With the blood you've lost, you will pass out for sure. Just lay there for a bit. Let me get you some smoked fish and more water."

"How long was I out? Stock inquired softly, trying to get some idea of what had happened since he came crashing through the doorway. The doorway, the gunshot, the doctor waving a white flag; his confusion now turned to anger.

"Doc, what da hell were you doin' standing in the doorway waving a white flag?" His raspy voice had a razor's edge; a tone that Andersen had not heard before. "You nearly got both of us killed."

Martin's face assumed the look of a crestfallen lad whose mother had discovered that he stole some candy from the local dry goods store. "I was afraid you had left me, Mr. Stock. So much time had passed. Not that I would have blamed you. This is not your business, and you have no duty to endanger your life for a man you've known for a single day. I was going to surrender, and take my chances. I didn't know what else to do."

"Surrender? Your brother ain't lookin' to take you prisoner. He's out to kill ya."

After his outburst, Stock's face softened a bit, but he was still upset: upset at the attacker who had invaded Stock's home; upset at the doctor for putting him in the line of fire, but mostly he was mad at himself for getting shot. He was a top notch woodsman and hunter, and he knew the land around these lakes like he knew the scars and lines on the back of his hands. How did this man get the drop on him?

"Ben, I saw him. I saw the man who shot you." Andersen was now standing over Stock, cradling a large slab of smoked lake trout in one hand, and his shiny white pillow in the other. He handed the fish to Ben as he propped up his head with the pillow. "He stood up when he saw you coming down the hill. That's when I grabbed the pistol and started shooting. I got a good look at him. It was not my brother!"

Ben lay quietly, gulping down the smoked fish. He was ravenous and the large piece of fish disappeared quickly. He drank more water, and slowly felt revived. The burning under his arm was painful, but tolerable. As he consumed the last tasty pieces of trout, Ben could only wonder, 'if it's not Martin's brother out there, than who?'

Chapter 23

Sheets of rain poured from the heavens as jagged bolts of lightning flashed across the sky. Thunder, like the roar of distant cannon, rumbled and echoed through pitch dark woods as Arlo Peterson and the caretaker finally arrived back at Camp. For the last half mile, the driving rain and booming thunder had spooked the horses. If not for the steady hands of caretaker Ben on the reins, it was likely the horses would have bolted, leaving the wagon and its passengers stranded, or worse.

As the wagon finally rolled to a stop in front of the lodge, Peterson jumped down and ran toward the building. He was soaked to the skin, chilled and hungry. "Take care of the horses," he yelled over his shoulder. A minute later he stomped into the great room. All heads turned in his direction.

"So?" Alan Prescott asked impatiently.

"Everything is taken care of," Peterson announced confidently while pulling off his soaked wool jacket, and tossing it on a chair. "Schmidt is headed to Duluth, and I sent a wire to Sheriff Chambers informing him of the accident."

A bright flash of light followed immediately by a sharp crack of thunder shook the building and the men's nerves. In the momentary silence, the pleasant and welcome smell of frying venison steaks floated into the great room. "Here Arlo, take this blanket," said Anders

Johnson. "You look like a drowned rat."

Peterson gratefully accepted the warm blanket and a tall glass of rye whiskey that Wentworth had poured for him. As the rain continued to pound on the cedar shingles, the men began to relax. Maybe this summer expedition would not be a total loss.

Outside, in the blinding rain, Ben unharnessed the horses, and prodded them into the stable. They were still jumpy from the rain and noise, and both were glad to be in a familiar place that was warm and dry. After leading each horse into their stall, he brought them fresh hay and a tin of oats. Ben had a special fondness for horses, and these two had done well getting them to town and back through the raging storm. Closing the stall gates, he turned to head out of the stable door when he found himself face to face with Anders Johnson.

"Mr. Johnson, whadda' you doing out here?" the caretaker asked, surprised to see any Venture Club member outside in weather like this. Ben had recognized early on, that while these men spoke of seeking harrowing wilderness adventures, it was mostly talk. They were city men.

The rain was beginning to ease, but thick clouds kept the stable shrouded in clammy darkness. "I needed some fresh air, Ben," Johnson said with hollow conviction.

The caretaker couldn't help but smile, thinking it odd that someone would come to a stable with wet horses and ripe manure in search of fresh air. Johnson, quickly recognizing that his answer sounded silly, smiled back. "Well, let's just say I needed to get out of the lodge for a while." Johnson continued to smile as he leaned up against one of the stalls. "Anyway, the cook is making supper, and I imagine you are starving after the day you've had."

Johnson, much more than the others, always made a point to treat the caretaker and cook with respect; even if they were hired men. Ben appreciated that, and gave Johnson a wide smile. "Must admit, my belly is pretty empty. Guess I'll head over." He nodded at Johnson as he made his way out the door and headed toward the lodge.

Johnson turned, watching as the caretaker disappeared into the side door. Looking around the dark stable, he located a couple of hay bales that provided him a comfortable spot to sit. Johnson grew up on a family farm, and actually enjoyed taking care of the livestock. To this day he missed caring for animals that took care of his family. As he sat comfortably on a sweet smelling bale of fresh hay, his thoughts wandered back to those simple, happy days in Goteborgs, Sweden. America, Minnesota, the City of Duluth had been good to Anders, but here in the stable he felt an agonizing pang of regret as he thought of his parents whom he would never see again. His brother had sent him a letter, now almost three years ago, informing him that their parents had passed away within just weeks of each other. How he wished that he could have seen them one more time…. but that was not to be.

It was then that he heard a low, eerie sound coming from the far corner of the stable where the shadows swallowed the faint light that crept into the building. Staring into the darkness, Anders saw what appeared to be a heavy dark horse blanket draped over several hay bales; and it appeared to be moving.

His first thought was that a wild animal had found refuge in the dry stable. Grabbing a pitchfork he found leaning against one of the stalls, Johnson approached the blanket with a mixture of fear and curiosity. But a moment later, a pair of hands emerged from within the thick blanket, pulling back the covering to reveal a thick shock of red hair.

"Sally," Johnson exclaimed, "what are you doing here?" He could now see the woman's hair was plastered on her head, most likely the result of being out in the heavy rain. Her eyes seemed to have a glazed, empty look, and she showed no sign of recognizing Anders.

Grabbing a kerosene lamp from a nearby hook, he lit the blackened wick with one hand while holding tight to the pitchfork in the other. As Johnson moved closer, the dark corner became illuminated. Even in the light the girl said nothing. Now as he stood over her, the light revealed that something was terribly wrong. Above her forehead, he could see thick clumps of what appeared to be dried blood mixed in with her orange-red hair; the pupils of her eyes were widely dilated. She made no attempt to talk, and simply stared straight ahead.

"Sally, can you hear me?" Johnson pleaded urgently, setting down the pitchfork, and placing his hand on her shoulder. "What happened to you?" At first there was no response, then Sally wet her lips as she tried to speak.

"I don't know," she muttered slowly.

Chapter 24

With darkness closing in, Dr. Martin Andersen and Benjamin Stock prepared for another night in the lodge. Stock was still lying on top of the table, growing increasingly impatient to get up and get going. At the same time a paralyzing wave of foreboding and fear had seized Martin. "Ben, what are we going to do?" he asked in a high pleading voice.

Stock ignored the question. "Doc, I gotta go."

Martin frowned and shook his head. "You can't go, you need to lie there, and rest."

"No, I mean I really gotta go. You been filling me up with water, you know. It gotta go somewhere."

A faint smile appeared on Martin's face. In light of all that had happened, and the imminent dangers that lurked outside, Ben continued to demonstrate a reassuring level of calm and courage Martin had rarely witnessed, nor ever experienced himself. Sarge was indeed a man to respect.

"OK, Mr. Stock, listen carefully. Don't try to stand up quickly, or you will black out for sure. I must help you. First, swing your legs over the side of the table." In obvious pain, Stock did as he was instructed.

With legs now dangling over the side of the table, Martin placed a firm hand on Stock's shoulder and slowly helped him sit upright. Almost immediately, Stock's face turned a pasty white and he began to perspire heavily. Staring straight ahead he felt like he was peering through a thick curtain of cobwebs. As he swayed back and forth, he fought to keep himself upright; looking like a young sapling in a windstorm. Fortunately, after a minute or two he felt himself relax, and his vision began to clear. He looked at the doctor and smiled.

"I'm gonna make it Doc."

Andersen was reassuring, "I know you are, Mr. Stock." With his arm firmly around Stock's waist, he guided them toward the far corner of the lodge where a large metal pail had been serving as their chamber pot for the last day. Once he had finished, Martin help steer Stock to his rocking chair. Relieved and relaxed in his favorite spot, Ben tried to unravel events of day.

"Doc, when I was passed out, I had the strangest dream." He paused for a moment, trying to sort out real images from the imagined. "I was in a small fishing boat with my Pap. The waves were fearsome. I was tryin' to strike the sail, when Pap yelled out that the girl was at the bottom of the lake."

Just then a low, unexpected groan, rattled through the lodge. Andersen felt his heart skip a beat, as he reached for his pistol and pointed it at the front door. Ben seemed totally unperturbed. "Ain't nothing, just some logs gettin' comfortable," he assured Martin. It was a moment or two before Andersen was convinced, and returned to their conversation.

"What girl?"

"Well that's just it….damnedest thing I ever seen….I look back and she's steering the boat."

"Who, what girl?" Andersen shot back, again wondering if Stock's wound and loss of blood had affected his brain as well as his arm.

"The girl who run off, after that German fellar drowned."

"She was at the bottom of the lake, and then she was steering your boat?" Martin was getting more confused by the minute.

"Just as pretty as you please; and doing a fine job if it, from what I can recall."

Andersen assigned little value to people's dreams or other whispered messages from the great beyond. Scientifically, it was pretty easy to attribute Stock's unusual recollections to his injury, and the stress they had both endured over the last 24 hours. While it seemed very real to Stock, Andersen was sure it was nothing more than a wild dream.

As he slowly rocked in his chair, Stock's thoughts wandered back to his getting shot. "You know what Doc.....I been going over it in my head, and I gotta believe there are two of them out there."

"What?" Andersen replied, unsure what 'two of them' Stock was referring.

"I seen a flash of metal from the raspberry thickets up the hill from the lodge. That's where I was goin' when the other varmint got the drop on me. That explains it." Stock stated firmly. "I think your brother brought a friend with him."

Martin considered the possibility that there were two men hunting him, hunting them. But that still didn't answer the most basic question of all. Why? Why was his brother, or anyone for that matter so desperate, or so...that they would take such chances and work so hard to kill him? What did he know, or what did he have... Suddenly he recalled thick sheaf of papers he had found when he had first arrived at the lodge.

"Ben, did you ever find a thick packet of papers, tied with a string in one of the cupboards?"

Stock, his eyes now nearly closed, stopped rocking. From the earnest look on his face, he appeared to be digging through the dark recesses of his memory trying to unearth the distant past. "Oh, yeh...you mean them papers in the locked compartment by the sink?"

Andersen nodded slowly, expecting more details. But obviously Stock had found little in the papers to interest him, either then or now, and offered no more on the subject. The thought did occur to Martin that maybe Ben could not read, and that was the reason for his uncaring attitude toward the papers.

Unable to slake his own curiosity, Andersen slid into the kitchen, carefully avoiding the bullet ridden window above the sink. Locating the hidden latch beneath the last cupboard, he gave it a pull. Again, the small door creaked open, revealing the tightly wrapped wad of papers.

Back in the great room, he sat at the pine table, now tarnished with bullet holes and blood stains. Placing one of the kerosene lamps on the table, he carefully loosened the tightly knotted string. He began to separate and examine the numerous sheets of paper that were folded into the bundle. He quickly noticed that all the pages were finely embossed with letterhead: **Wentworth and Associates Duluth Minnesota**. All of the letters were addressed to Thomas Schmidt, and seemed to relate to business dealings and offers for representation and legal counsel.

"There is nothing here, certainly nothing worth dying for" Andersen said loudly, but only to himself as Ben was now snoring noisily. Martin smiled for a moment, and then frowned. An icy wave of guilt washed over him, fed by the pain he had brought to this simple, good-hearted man. Regrettably, it was quite likely that the potential for greater harm lurked in the dark woods beyond their barricaded doors.

Chapter 25

In 1881, a deadly typhoid epidemic struck the city of Duluth. In response, Reverend J.A. Cummings opened the city's first hospital, St. Luke's, in an old blacksmith shop sparsely furnished with three beds, and a stove donated by British officials at the Duluth emigrant station. Three years later the hospital was relocated to a larger space at the corner of 2nd Avenue and 4th Street that could accommodate thirty-eight beds. As the population boom continued, demand for modern hospital care grew with it. In 1902, the latest manifestation of St. Luke's was completed. With 85 beds for the ill and injured, the new building displayed no pretense, nuance or architectural style. It was an unremarkable four story cheese box designed for treating the sick and saving lives; nothing more.

As chief surgeon for the city's largest hospital, Dr. Martin Andersen found that serving the role of county coroner came with the job. It was not something he much liked; he was much more interested in saving lives then trying to discover why some left this life behind, but as with all things, he performed the duty with skill and dedication. With its boom town status creating a steady influx of immigrants, including a fair share of shysters, thieves and con men, unexpected and unsavory forms of death were as common as the smoke-belching steamers that paraded back and forth along the Duluth waterfront.

His tiny office was located on the fourth floor of St. Luke's, and its lone window peered out on 1st Street in downtown Duluth. Two blocks up from the waterfront, the busy thoroughfare beneath his window had recently been paved with tight rows of knobby cobblestone which now caused a ferocious racket as fleets of horse drawn steel-wheeled wagons, buggies and all manner of conveyance clomped past the hospital. At busy times of the day, Andersen sometimes wondered if trading mud for that unholy racket was a good bargain.

The morning sun was veiled by a thick layer of creamy white fog that floated in from the lake. It was not unusual for it to take several hours before the summer sun could burn away that layer, but for now it provided an eerie, damp feel to the downtown. Just enough light streamed in through the narrow window behind Andersen's desk that he found no need to switch on the new incandescent electric light bulbs that been recently installed in the hospital.

The Duluth News Tribune headline for July 13, 1912 barked out news about the raging fire that had incinerated several large warehouses along the waterfront the previous day. Propelled by a nasty south wind, the fire had raged uncontained for several hours, before running out of structures to consume. Thick, choking smoke had filled the downtown area but amazingly, no one had been killed or injured; a surprise blessing for a town that seemed to have a penchant for discovering novel and numerous ways to kill off its residents.

Sitting quietly in his office, Dr. Andersen scanned the morning paper which he had purchased from the ambitious newsboy who seemed to be perpetually stationed outside the entrance to the hospital.

As always, Andersen had flipped the boy a dime for the nickel broadsheet, eliciting a wide smile from the appreciative lad. Just then, the doorway of his office was filled with a shadow that remained motionless and silent. Looking up from his paper, Dr. Andersen greeted his visitor. "Sheriff Chambers, what gets you out of bed so early on this fine morning?"

St. Louis County Sheriff Willis Chambers was a mountain of a man. As tall as the door frame and nearly as wide, he was intimidating if only because of his size. His face was round and jowly, decorated with a thick 'soup strainer' moustache that nearly hid his mouth and often provided clues to what the Sheriff had for dinner. His uniform cap, which was smashed low on his head, barely contained the wild crop of jet black hair that covered his head, and hung down below his ears. His small, deep-set brown eyes looked out of place on his large face and to those he met it appeared that he was perpetually squinting.

"Doc, can I talk to you for a minute?' Chambers asked cautiously, as he reached up to remove his cap.

"Certainly Sheriff, please, come in, sit down."

Andersen had first met Chambers three years ago, when he had been elected Sheriff. His election had come as a surprise to many residents, especially as he bested a well-regarded incumbent. Chambers was a decent sort, no one in town disputed that, but he was viewed by more than a few as something of a rube; slightly slow and unsophisticated. After the election, rumors circulated that Arlo Peterson, owner of Comstock-Peterson Logging Co. had played an influential and possibly illicit role in getting Chambers elected.

Chambers collapsed into the lone chair set in front of Andersen's desk, laid his cap on the edge of the desk and with both hands tried to coax his unruly hair from his eyes. "Doc, I got a wire last night from Arlo Peterson. You know 'em?" Chambers seemed more nervous than usual as he wrapped his enormous hands tightly around the arms of the chair, as if at any minute the chair was about to catapult itself across the room.

"I know the name, of course," Andersen replied slowly. "But I've never met the man."

"Well, he sent me a wire last night…seems a fellow named Thomas Schmidt, one of the owners of the Duluth and Northern Minnesota Railroad drowned yesterday. I guess there was a group of them, all local business men, at some fishing camp way up the shore. Arlo, eh, Mr. Peterson said it was accidental; guess the man was drinking a lot, wandered off in the dark, and they found him next morning floating in the lake."

Outside of Andersen's window a procession of heavily loaded wagons clattered by. Andersen slowly folded the newspaper in half, and placed it on the corner of his desk. "Does anyone dispute those facts, Sheriff?"

"Not that I know of."

"Where is the body now?"

"Mr. Peterson said he was sending the body by rail from Lax Lake down to the Fjedheim Mortuary over on London Road."

"Sheriff, right now I have three bodies in the morgue that need to be examined. As you well know, people drowning here is not uncommon. From what you have told me, this does not appear to require an autopsy."

"Doc, I agree with you, but…."

"But what Sheriff?" Andersen looked up, suddenly more interested than before. "Is there something you haven't told me?"

Chambers wove his fingers together behind his head, and slowly rocked back in the office chair, which groaned loudly in protest. "Doc, a couple a days ago, I got a letter claiming that Thomas Schmidt's life was in danger, that someone was out to kill him."

Andersen stared deeply into the Sheriff's beady, badger eyes. "Do you have any idea who sent the letter?"

"Pretty sure. It was on D&NMR stationary, and it was signed by Thomas Schmidt."

Chapter 26

As he hovered over Sally, peering down into her open but empty eyes, Anders Johnson was at a loss for what he should do. Had Sally somehow fallen, hitting her head, causing the blood and her nearly unconscious condition, or had she been attacked by someone here at the Camp. Did Thomas Schmidt have something to do with this? Without Sally's help, it was very likely he would never find out.

Johnson softly patted her cheek. "Sally, Sally," he spoke with calm, comforting voice. Her eyes were fixed, without movement or depth. Occasionally her eyelids would flicker, and then close very slowly. There was no sign that she knew where she was, or even who she was.

Glancing around the stable, Johnson spotted a pail filled with lake water. Taking a cloth from a nearby hook, he dipped it into the cool water, soaking it completely. Wringing it out, he slowly and carefully dabbed at Sally's face and forehead, wiping away the blood and dirt that clung there. Though he swabbed her face and head as gently as he could, she would wince occasionally as the cool water found a raw spot on her face or scalp. Slowly, her eyes began to regain some focus, and she now appeared to be aware of Johnson's good Samaritan-like work, though without comment. Once finished, Johnson soaked and wrung the cloth one last time before laying it gently on her forehead. He sat back on the hay bale. Time and the soothing result of the water appeared to be having a good effect.

"Thank you Mr. Johnson," Sally said weakly, slowly turning her head to look directly at him. Johnson smiled sweetly, and reached out his hand, gently stroking Sally's cheek.

"You're going to be alright." He said with a tone that was part question and part encouragement. "Can you remember anything? Who did this to you?" He asked, eager to learn what had happened.

Sally turned her head away. Her eyelids opened and closed rapidly, as she attempted to hold back tears while trying to retrieve hidden memories from the deep recesses of her subconscious.

"I found Hannah..... hiding," she offered with a surprising nonchalance.

"Hiding? They said she had run off."

Johnson was suddenly confused. Though he was not yet certain if Sally was clear-headed enough to recall what had actually happened, he began to wonder if some of the others were not telling the truth. "Do you remember anything else?"

Sally slowly closed her eyes and held them tightly shut for several seconds. Without opening them, she began to recite the events that brought her to this place.

"I tricked the other men, Billy and Mr. Wentworth," she relayed without a hint of remorse. "I found Hannah but I told them that she had run off. They were happy to believe me." Sally stopped, and slowly licked her lips. She opened her eyes, and turned her head to look directly at Johnson. "Someone must have followed me back to the lake." Tears now filled her eyes, and a rivulet cascaded down each cheek. "I fear that poor Hannah is dead."

Chapter 27

With the sun now a faint memory in the western sky, the interior of the lodge was nearly dark. The only light came from the soft glow of the smoldering fire in the fireplace and one kerosene lamp that Andersen had placed next to him on the pine table. Stock, his head tilted back, slept deeply, snoring loudly in his rocking chair, his rifle lay across his legs, his right hand firmly encircling the trigger guard. Martin sat at the table, gnawing idly on a large chunk of dried venison while poring through the stack of papers he had found in the cupboard. Next to him, within easy reach, was his pistol, loaded and cocked.

As he examined the documents more carefully, he began to sense that what was written carried more meaning than the words expressed. The letters were similar in content; each of them described some legal service or consul that John Wentworth had, or was going to provide. And each of the letters ended with a similar closing that stated '..per our standing agreement, there will be no charge for this service.' Letter by letter, Martin read this comment time and again, with growing interest.

'What would that agreement be?' he thought to himself. These letters had to important to someone. There must be some reason they were bundled together and hid at Tettegouche Camp. Was it some 'under the table' transaction, or maybe blackmail? Martin had to find out. Suddenly, the snoring stopped, and Stock began to fidget in the chair. His eyes flickered open, and he wiped the palms of his hands across his face.

"How long have I been out?" he asked with a surprising touch of disgust.

"A couple of hours."

"What time is it?"

Andersen pulled his watch from his pocket, wondering himself what time it was. "It's almost 9:00 o'clock, Mr. Stock."

Ben rubbed his eyes and sat forward in his rocking chair. "What are you looking at, Doc," he asked trying to get caught up.

Andersen described the contents of the letters, and the puzzling line about a 'standing agreement' while Stock listened without comment. "Mr. Stock, can you remember if there was any sort of rub between Schmidt and Wentworth; anything that would indicate that Schmidt had some kind of hold over Wentworth?"

Stock rocked back in his chair staring wistfully up into the rafters of the lodge. For a moment he was silent, and then slowly a long buried recollection emerged.

"I was out tending the horses, pretty sure it was the first night we arrived, back in the summer of '12," he replied slowly assembling scattered fragments from his memory. "It was getting dark and I hear voices from behind the stable. As I think about it now, I'm sure it was the German and that young lawyer. Schmidt was laying into Wentworth pretty good, saying something like 'if you don't take care of business, I will find someone else to partner with.'"

"Mr. Wentworth was saying, 'don't worry about it, I'll take care of it.' But Schmidt kept right on threatening him, saying he would ruin him." Stock stopped rocking and rubbed his arm. "That's it.... that's all I can remember about them two."

Just then, a soft thumping noise penetrated the far end of the lodge. Andersen grabbed for his pistol, and Stock sat up ramrod straight in his chair holding his rifle in a military forward arms position. It sounded like something was being thrown against the outside wall and continued for many minutes.

"What is it?" Andersen whispered as a soft orange glow began to reflect and shimmer through the window in the middle of the wall opposite the fireplace.

"I was afraid this might happen," Stock said with an eerie resignation. "They're gonna burn us out."

Chapter 28

For Sally, the slow grinding ride back from Tettegouche Camp was unbearable torture. Her head was pounding and her ears rang as the wagon, driven by the caretaker, banged and crawled its way to Lax Lake. Ben and Einar sat on the driver's bench, while Sally and the other girls sat on side benches facing each other in the bed of the wagon.

During the long trip, the girls said nothing to Sally; it was clear that something dreadful had happened to her. Her usually rosy cheeks were pale, her face drawn. Her bright green eyes were barely open, and seemed vacant, unfocused. Not sure who she could trust, Sally had said nothing to the girls about the attack and her condition. Anders Johnson, who had helped her from the stable to woman's sleeping quarters, had kept quiet about what he knew. When asked by several of the Venture Club members, Sally stuck to the story that Hannah had run off; fully aware that the killer among them would know that Sally was lying; a convenient and painful lie.

Finally after several dreadful hours, they arrived back at the Duluth train depot. A horse drawn cab waited to collect the men and their baggage to ferry them to their homes. The women were expected to fend for themselves. As the cab pulled away from the depot, Peterson yelled to the women that they would be notified by messenger when their services would next be required.

Sally lived in tiny room on the upper floor of a boarding house located on 3nd Street, straight up the hill from the train depot. The other girls, who lived near the waterfront, bid Sally a sad goodbye as they headed down the hill. Carrying her grip, she began to trudge the five blocks up the steep grade. It was an unusually warm, late afternoon in Duluth, tempered only slightly by a cool breeze riding in from the lake. Soon Sally was perspiring heavily, feeling dizzy; almost disconnected from her body. Her long dress swept the ground as she passed Superior Street. By the time she reached 2nd St. her breathing became labored, her head felt like it was going to explode. It was then that she began to feel sick to her stomach and a moment later she was bent over, vomiting in the middle of the street. A moment after that she was unconscious, lying on the cold damp cobblestones.

She felt herself floating above the tree tops, soaring like the bald eagles so common along the hilltops surrounding the city of Duluth. But below her were not streets and buildings, but lakes and trees. She recognized the she was circling over Tettegouche Camp; the lodge and bunkhouses, and the lakes that surrounded them. A dazzling clear blue sky enveloped her; with nary a hint of clouds in any direction. As she floated, she felt calm and relaxed. There was no headache or pain of any kind. She wondered, without apprehension, if she had died. If so, she was at peace with that. Life had been tough; death might provide a welcome release.

But then, the warm breezes that had kept her soaring without effort, ceased. She struggled to stay aloft, but felt herself falling, falling, gaining speed and heading directly toward Tettegouche Lake. A moment later, she awoke, drenched and freezing.

"Miss. Miss. Can you hear me?"

Sally opened her eyes, and for an instant was not sure if she was alive or dead. The room, if it was indeed a room and not some way station on the road to the pearly gates was pasty white, brightly lit and morbidly sterile. She was laying on something as hard and cold as iron.

"Miss, can you hear me?"

As her eyes slowly adapted to the blazing lights, Sally gazed up at a handsome, middle-aged man with bright blue eyes and a furrowed brow. Except for his neatly trimmed goatee, she realized that she was staring at Matts Andersen. Confused, and suddenly frightened, she spoke plaintively. "Mr. Andersen? What are you doing here?"

The man appeared surprised, and responded calmly, "Do I know you?"

"Of course you do. We just spent three days...." suddenly, Sally stopped. The thought now struck her that Matts Andersen may have been her attacker and he was back to finish the job. She tried to sit upright, but the man with a bright white knee length duster placed his hands firmly on her shoulders, pinning her to the table.

"Help me, Help!" she screamed.

Out of nowhere, a plain-looking woman, wearing an immaculate white dress, with a starched white bonnet appeared. Together they were able to hold Sally down on the table. The severe pounding in her head returned, and she slumped back; unable to resist, ready to accept her fate. "What did you do with Hannah?" she hissed, hoping to at least find out what happened to the young girl, before they did the same to her.

In a soft, soothing voice the man asked. "Who is Hannah?"

"The girl you...." She stopped before she could finish the sentence.

With her eyes now wide open, Sally could see the man and the woman dressed like an angel exchange odd glances. "Miss, it appears you suffered a nasty blow to the head. Based on what happened out in the street, you likely have a severe concussion, possibly a skull fracture. I am going to admit you to the hospital for several days, so we can monitor your health."

Sally was now even more confused. "Where am I?"

"You're in St. Luke's Hospital, miss. And somehow you know my name. But I am a doctor." Martin said softly. "What is your name?"

Confused, fearful, racked by pain and guilt, the girl replied slowly, "Me name is Sally Keefe."

Chapter 29

In 1909, Marshall Alworth, a wealthy industrialist who made several fortunes in the timber and land business in northeastern Minnesota, put up the money to construct Duluth's tallest building; the tallest this side of Chicago.

Higher than any in Minneapolis or Saint Paul, and a scant 35 feet shy of the tallest in New York City, the Alworth Building soared a mind boggling 247 feet into the air. The sixteen-story 'skyscraper', as buildings that achieved such dizzying heights were now known, was located on West Superior Street, just two blocks from the waterfront. Built in the Chicago School style, the entire building was wrapped in a coat of light brown brick. In pleasing contrast to the rectangular windows located in the floors below, the top floor featured large ornately carved oval windows, each topped with a lion's head sculpture.

Looking out from one of its oval windows, Arlo Peterson's massive office provided breathtaking panoramas of the Duluth harbor, and the gritty port city below. Having just returned from Tettegouche Camp, Peterson sat at his magnificent hand carved walnut desk catching up on business. As he poured over a series of financial reports and contracts, a soft knock on the door interrupted his concentration. "Come in," he said curtly. Peterson's office girl, Edna, opened the door just wide enough to pop in her head.

"Mr. Peterson, Sheriff Chambers is here to see you. He doesn't have an appointment. Should I tell him to come back later?"

"No, no, send him right in," Peterson said energetically as he took off his eye glasses and uncharacteristically stood to greet his visitor.

Holding his crumpled uniform hat in his hands, Willis Chambers appeared in the doorway looking like a man who was taking his final steps toward the gallows. Peterson offered Chambers his hand, greeting him warmly.

"Sheriff, good to see you! Thanks for stopping by. Edna please close the door," Peterson said with an uncommonly gracious nod toward his office girl. "Please, Sheriff sit down, take a load off your feet. Can I offer you something to drink?" Peterson waved his arm toward a nearby sideboard that displayed an impressive array of distilled spirits.

"No, no thank you, Mr. Peterson." Chambers sat down heavily in the chair as he continued to strangle his cap.

Peterson sat back in his brown leather chair. He was a man who invested little time in social banter and quickly got to the issue that most concerned him. "Sheriff, I am assuming you're here related to the unfortunate matter concerning Thomas Schmidt?" Chambers stopped torturing his cap, and nodded. "I am also assuming that all has been taken care of, and the matter is now settled?"

"Well…" Chambers cleared his throat, searching for the right words; certain that he was about to deliver some unwelcomed news. "The coroner says that an autopsy must be done." Chambers resumed twisting his cap, as he stole a glance up at Peterson.

"What?" Peterson roared, his face instantly becoming a tart cherry red. This was not what he expected to hear from the man for whom he had done so much. The color faded quickly however, as Peterson was well practiced at managing his fiery temper and quickly recaptured his composure. He placed the palms of his hands on top of his desk and stood up, moving slowly and deliberately around the desk before sitting on the edge of the desk directly in front of Chambers. Peterson glared directly into Sheriff Chambers deeply set eyes, and spoke with a controlled calm, carefully enunciating each word.

"Sheriff, I told you this was an unfortunate accident; nothing more. We need to bury this poor fellow as soon as possible. Do you understand what I am saying?"

Peterson was now leaning forward, his face no more than a foot from Chambers. His arms were crossed firmly in front of him. Chambers could feel beads of sweat forming along the back of his neck, which would soon start rolling down his back. For a moment he wanted to reveal to Peterson the letter from Schmidt expressing fear for his life, but Doctor Andersen had asked him to keep that bit of information to himself.

"Mr. Peterson, it's out of my hands. The coroner says he won't issue a death certificate 'til he figures out the cause of death, and the funeral parlor won't process and bury the body 'til they got one."

Peterson stood, walked slowly over to the sideboard, and poured himself a small tumbler of scotch whiskey. Taking a deep sip, he cradled the heavy glass in both hands, considering his next move.

"Who did you say the county coroner was again?"

"Doctor Martin Andersen, over at St. Luke's."

"Oh, yes, that's right. Andersen." Petersen smiled as he remembered that he had one more card to play.

Chapter 30

Andersen was stunned. "Burn us out?" he croaked, with a combination of disbelief and terror. Suddenly it felt like two icy hands were gripping him tightly around the windpipe. "What are we going to do?" His heart was pounding and his legs seemed intent on racing for the door.

Awkwardly, Stock struggled to his feet, unsteady but determined. As he walked toward the far wall, he could see that the flames were already reaching the height of the window. Though the night was cool and damp, he was certain that it would not take long before the pile of limbs that the attackers must have placed up against the outside wall would ignite the old white pine logs. Once that happened the lodge would become a fiery maelstrom.

Terrified, Martin grabbed his pistol from the table and leveled it at the front door. "We've got to make a run for it, Ben!"

"Doc, that's what their wantin' us to do," Stock said calmly. "Them coyotes probably got both doors covered, and soon as we show our faces.... its good night Mary."

"Well, it worked before when I provided cover while you made it out the back, can we try that again?" Martin could feel himself becoming lightheaded, entering an almost dreamlike state. For a moment he wondered if it just a nightmare.

"Won't work now," Stock reasoned. "It's dark, and they know we gotta come out or be cooked alive. Everything's in their favor."

The flames from the swiftly growing fire were now reaching over the top of the window, and several of the larger logs near the middle of the wall were beginning to smoke; the growing blaze driving off what little moisture remained in the old logs.

Unexpectedly, Andersen now felt a keen sense of remorse; the guilt of putting Mr. Stock in this situation weighed almost as heavily on his conscience as uncontrollable fear did to his mind. All he could think to do was to apologize; for whatever good that might do.

"Mr. Stock, I am so sorry for the scourge I have brought upon you." The blue-tinted .45 now hung from his right arm like a boat anchor.

Stock, inexplicably smiled a broad toothy smile, as he gazed confidently at the good doctor. "We ain't cooked yet Doc."

Having been around during the construction of the Camp buildings and for some years since, Stock was keenly aware of the unique elements of the buildings that formed Tettegouche Camp. One was that all the buildings were set on rubble stone foundations.

Rubble stone foundations are composed of handpicked, neatly arranged rows of stone or rock held together with small amounts of mason cement. Though not elegant, these foundations formed a solid base upon which the logs were set. At the Camp, rubble stone foundations ran the entire length of each building except for the area under the lodge's enormous fireplace. Here, due to the crushing weight of the tons of stone and granite used to fabricate the mammoth fireplace, a three foot thick, reinforced footing of sand, gravel and portland cement had been laid down by the masons.

Over the last couple years, Stock had noticed that where the foundation met this immovable concrete footing, the remarkable ability of freezing and thawing water to destroy man's handiwork; be it the cobblestone streets of Minneapolis, or the ornate stonework in downtown Duluth, had wrenched a number of stones loose from the foundation. This created an opening into the narrow crawlspace that lay under the wood floors of the lodge. Stock remembered he had been vexed by the thought of an unwanted roommate; a sleepy black bear looking for a cozy retreat to hibernate for the winter, finding that opening. However, he had never worried enough to do anything about it.

Stock tried to explain all this to Martin, who saw no need to learn about the construction of the lodge. In frustration, Andersen lost control, and his fear-inspired rage boiled over. "Who gives a damn about all that, you son-of-a bitch. If we don't get out of here, we are going to burn to death."

As soon the words escaped his lips, Andersen felt a sharp stab of shame, wishing he could reach out and retrieve his callous comments before they entered Ben's ears. Of course, he could not. He frowned and meekly apologized. "I'm so sorry Mr. Stock, I'm terrified that we are going to die."

Stock's easy smile immediately palliated Martin's feelings. "Don't worry 'bout it Doc, I been called some worse."

The logs directly above the fire were now smoking profusely, filling the upper levels of the lodge with a thick cloud of acrid smoke. Stoically, Andersen realized that it would probably be the smoke and lack of oxygen that would kill them long before the flames incinerated their bodies. He wasn't sure if that was a better fate, but from the flurry of activity that now possessed Stock, it was clear he had no intention of dying from either.

Vigorously, Stock dug through his footlocker and extracted a number of items. First, was his double-barreled shotgun, which Andersen had seen up close the night before. Digging deeper, he retrieved a handful of shotgun shells. He then scrounged an old leather holster, which he snugged tightly around his waist. Grabbing the pistol from Andersen's sweaty grip, he released the hammer into the safety position and slid it into the holster as he pocketed the last remaining clip. "Here Doc, you take the scattergun," Stock directed. As he did, he took a minute to show Andersen how the lever on top of the stock flipped sideways, cracking open the gun to expose the breech. He slid a shell into each barrel and snapped the gun shut.

"When you're ready to fire, pull the hammers back til they lock in place." Stock instructed. Andersen was more concerned about billowing plumes of smoke now filling the lodge then more terse lessons on firearms. He nodded solemnly without really listening. "The front trigger fires the left barrel, and the back trigger the right. Whatever, you do, don't pull them at the same time. Got it?"

Martin was confused, but more anxious to get going. "Sure, I got it."

"With that old blunderbuss, you ain't gotta be too accurate…a couple of blasts of ten gauge double-0 buckshot will take out a small posse." A devious, childlike smile blossomed on Stock's face.

Next he took out a box of 30-30 cartridges and filled the magazine of Winchester rifle. Finally, he pulled out a long bladed knife, which Andersen guessed was a military issue bayonet.

140

Suddenly, the logs on the far wall began to sizzle and pop, as the superheated gases began to split the logs like overripe tomatoes. A moment later, light blue flames began to dance upward on the inside wall of the cabin. Time was running short.

"Ready Doc?" Stock stood up, with his rifle in one hand and the bayonet in the other. "Grab that lantern; gets mighty dark in the crawlspace."

Martin was starting to understand Stock's plan, but considered it a desperate and reckless affair. He thought about stating his objection, but with no ready option in mind, he reluctantly followed Ben into the kitchen. There, Stock dropped to his knees under the sink, and using the point of his bayonet pried opened a small trapdoor that had been put there in case the well or drain pipes that ran beneath the lodge ever needed maintenance. The crackling fire began to roar like a wounded bear. Smoke billowed into the lodge, and the thick toxic layer was descending at an alarming rate; head high and dropping.

"Give me the lantern," Stock yelled, nearly ripping it from Martin's outstretched hand. Reaching down through the hole in the floor, he carefully set it on the cold, wet earth that lay beneath the lodge. "Follow me," Stock instructed, and despite his painful wound, slid headfirst into the hole as effortlessly as a fox enters its den. In just a few seconds his feet disappeared, and with him the light began to dim. Fighting a sudden wave of claustrophobia as he cradled the loaded shotgun, Andersen prepared to follow Stock into the darkness.

Suddenly, Stock's head popped back out of the opening like a curious ground squirrel, sending a jolt down Andersen's spine. "Jesus, Ben. What in the hell are you doing?"

141

Without a word, Stock climbed out of the hole, laid his rifle and bayonet on the floor, and sprinted into the great room. The deadly layer of smoke was now less than four feet from the floor forcing Sarge to run in a deep crouch to keep his head immersed in what little oxygen remained in their slowly closing coffin.

A moment after he disappeared, a purlin, one of the large logs that support the rafters on each side of the roof, broke away, crashing to the floor with a sickening thud. "Stock, are you alright!" Andersen bellowed. He was greeted with nothing but the sharp crackling and popping of incinerating wood and the ominous knell of a slowly disintegrating structure.

Chapter 31

"Mr. Peterson, Matts Andersen is here to see you," Edna announced softly through the partially opened door to his office in the Alworth Building.

"Thanks Edna, please show him in."

Matts Andersen nodded politely to the office girl as he passed into Peterson's palatial office. Arlo appeared almost tiny sitting behind the massive desk, a pair of wire-rimmed eyeglasses balanced precipitously on the end of this nose.

He glanced up from his papers and gave Andersen a welcoming nod. It had been through their mutual connection to Leonidas Merritt that Matts had become a member of the Venture Club. Merritt, forever attempting to thrust Matts to some advantage, had asked Peterson, as a personal favor, to invite Andersen to join. Though Arlo did not know the young man, he agreed as a favor to his fellow business titan. Since joining the Club, Arlo had been little impressed with Andersen's skills and ambition; it appeared that the rumors around town that Merritt was Matts' benefactor were most likely true.

"So good of you to come by on short notice, Matts, please sit down." Peterson removed his eye glasses tossing them idly on his desk, as he rocked back in his overstuffed brown leather chair. Peterson pointed toward the well-stocked sideboard, "Drink?" Though

Peterson's tone and mood seemed welcoming, Matts was on edge, certain that this was not to be a social visit.

"No thanks, Mr. Peterson," Matts replied hesitantly.

"Matts, please, sit."

Andersen slid into one of the two oaken chairs that were positioned in front of the desk. The palms of his hands were now sweaty. Embarrassed, he hoped Peterson would not offer his hand to him. He did not. Peterson did not dawdle, moving quickly to the issue at hand.

"This morning I had a conversation with County Sheriff Chambers. Do you know him?" Andersen shook his head slowly trying to anticipate where the conversation was going.

"Well, anyway, Sheriff Chambers told me that your brother, over at St. Luke's has decided that he is going to conduct an autopsy on poor Mr. Schmidt, despite all the information we gave him to prove that this was simply an unfortunate accident."

Andersen shifted uneasily in his chair, again nodding his head as he began to get the drift of Peterson's concerns. "Well, Mr. Peterson, since we all agree that this was an accident, there should be nothing to be concerned about, even if my brother does the autopsy."

Peterson leaned forward in this chair, clasping his hands together tightly before setting them firmly on the desktop. He spoke in a low tone, his voice nearly a whisper.

"There is something you need to know, something I have not told anyone." Peterson stopped for a moment, lacing and unlacing his fingers together. "I have some information that leads me to believe that one of the Venture Club members may have been involved

144

in Schmidt's death."

"What?" Andersen was shocked by the accusation. Why would anyone want to kill the German? As he slid back in his chair, he could not swallow the question that now escaped from his lips. "Who?"

"Well, I can't get into the details, but let's just say I am aware of some things that point in that direction."

"Well, shouldn't we pass that information along to the Sheriff?"

"Well, maybe……maybe," Peterson replied slowly. "But there might be more involved than just a moment of anger or revenge.

Andersen was now very confused. He eyed Peterson carefully for a hint of what those other things might be; but no clue was forthcoming. He was about to ask another question when Arlo jumped to his feet, eager to get the business over. "Matts, we…..you need to talk to your brother and convince him that an autopsy is unnecessary; a waste of time and money. And that he needs to declare this an accidental death, and issue the death certificate so we can bury this poor man and get back to business. Do you understand what I'm saying?"

As Peterson talked, he made his way around to the front of the desk and now stood next to Matts; still seated in his chair. He placed a heavy hand on Andersen's shoulder. It was now becoming clear, that what began as a request was now a command that Peterson expected be carried out, or there would be serious consequences.

Peterson repeated his question. "Do you understand what I am saying Matts?" He spoke deliberately and forcefully leaving no doubt in Matts' mind what he was saying.

"I'll, I'll, I'll talk to him," Andersen stuttered. "But... but I can't guarantee anything." Peterson's hand began to feel like a blacksmith's vice crushing his shoulder.

"Don't let us down," Peterson hissed.

Chapter 32

"Stock, are you alright?" Andersen yelled again; though he was pretty sure that his voice was being drowned out by the crackling, snapping inferno that was growing angrier by the minute. Billows of brown-gray smoke and superheated gases were now only a few feet above the floor. In was becoming obvious that just minutes remained before the poisonous air would begin to fill their lungs.

Then, through the smoke-filled doorway Ben appeared like an apparition; crouching low and moving fast. In his hands were the first aid kit and the package of papers that Martin had found in the cupboard. He put them both into the small knapsack that he slung over his shoulder. With a giant grin, Stock looked at the dumbfounded doctor. "What are ya waitin' for, let's get outta here. Stay close, and be quick about it"

As he had done moments before, Stock slipped down the hole, with ease. The roar of the fire was growing, and pieces of the roof supports were starting to peel away, slamming into the floor with an ominous thud as long tongues of fire began to reach into the kitchen.

Andersen got down on his hands and knees. Holding on to the edge of the trap door with one hand, he lowered his head and torso into the hole so he could lay the shotgun onto the ground. Now planting that hand on the wet earth, he released his grip on the edge of the opening and crawled into the abyss. He was greeted by a rank musty odor of mold and rotting wood which filled his nostrils. As he squirmed along on his belly, he could see the dim light of the lantern bobbing in front of him as Stock slithered toward the far end of the building. Above their heads the sounds of the inferno was growing more intense, and occasionally a massive log would slam the floor above their heads as more pieces of the roof's interior structure fell.

Fortunately the air in the crawl space, though stale and foul was cool and breathable. Weighed down by the heavy shotgun and his nearly paralyzing fear of small, dark spaces, Martin forced himself deeper into the narrow, suffocating darkness; driven by the knowledge that to stop meant death. The light of Stock's lantern was his only focus. It was his lighthouse, his guide to safety, and he knew that if the light disappeared, so would his courage, and ultimately, his life. As he crawled deeper into the inky darkness, his mind conjured up visions of snakes, and all sorts of creatures living and dead, lurking in the dark.

Finally, the light stopped moving, and Martin could hear Stock rustling through his knapsack. Crawling closer he watched as Stock took out his bayonet, and began to pry away at the loose stones that lay against an enormous concrete block. Above their heads, suddenly, inevitably, the fire opened a hole in the roof, allowing oxygen-rich outside air to be sucked into the oxygen deprived blaze within. Firemen referred to this phenomenon as a flash-over, and with a terrifying whoosh and muffled explosion, nearly the entire structure burst into flames. Less than a minute later, the ridgepole buckled, and chunks of flaming log and roof boards rained down onto the floor, punching holes through the thick pine floor boards. The stately lodge was following the path of all living things, ashes to ashes, dust to dust.

In the crawl space below, it created sights and sounds one could imagine if they were to witness the apocalypse. The floor above them was growing hot to the touch, and both of them were perspiring heavily. Undaunted, Stock frantically hacked and pried away at the stones, trying to create an opening large enough for them to slide through. Finally, it was ready. "OK, Doc, follow me. If they see us, we may have to stand and fight. Otherwise, stay low and run your ass off."

Stock pushed his rifle and backpack through the small hole in front of him, and then squeezed into the tight opening with a grunt. With some effort, he was able to wriggle through. As soon as his feet cleared, Andersen did the same. The moment Martin stuck his head through the hole it felt as if he had passed through the gates of hell. The blazing lodge lit up the sky brighter than a dozen mid-day suns. And though this end of the lodge was not yet fully involved, the heat was blistering. Martin felt almost naked as crawled away from the lodge, before leaping to his feet, and racing after Stock.

They ran toward the darkness, hoping their attackers were so intent on covering the doorways on either side of the lodge, that their escape would go undetected. As they reached the ring of shadows that hovered beyond the reach of the light from the blazing lodge, Stock stopped and dove into a small patch of young cedar trees. Martin followed him, finding a spot on the cold soft ground. Both were panting heavily, fighting to catch their breath, and gather their wits.

As Martin lay there, gulping in the cool night air, he began to wonder; is this the end of it, or just the beginning?

Chapter 33

The slowly disappearing summer sun cast long shadows over the city street below as Dr. Martin Andersen attacked the mountain of paperwork that continually accumulated on his desk. Like most days, it had been a non-stop series of scheduled surgeries, emergencies, patient visits and autopsies. He was tired, and eager to go home. As he leaned back in his chair, stretching his arms above his head, he was startled to see himself, standing silently in the doorway.

"Hello, Martin, may I come in?" asked Matts breezily. For several seconds there was a silence so oppressive, that the usually imperceptible ticking of the wall clock, seemed to echo through the room. Martin was tempted to say what was in his mind, which was 'no, go away', but reluctantly he nodded toward the chair in front of his desk.

Whenever the two brothers were alone together, there was always a fidgety, awkward silence. Neither was proficient at small talk, nor did they really have anything to talk about, except for their parents. In recent years the two rarely spoke; except at their parents home, or when Matts needed something. Martin was fully expecting the later was the reason for Matts visit, so he was the first to break the silence.

"What can I do for you, Matts?" His tone was flat, business-like.

Matts tried to ease into the reason for his visit. "How are you, Martin. I haven't seen you in quite a while?" Martin provided a curt 'fine' but did not follow it up with any customary pleasantries. Trying again to relax the frosty mood, Matts asked, "have you seen Ma and Pa recently?"

"Yes," Martin shot back. "Have you?"

Matts sat down in the chair, deciding whether to just leap into the reason he had come. But first, he had to get something off his chest. "Why do you hate me so much? What have I ever done to make you treat me this way?"

Martin was surprised by Matts' candor. Could he, should he explain to his twin brother why he felt such disgust for him. He would not even try. But Matts kept pushing the stone up the hill.

"Whether you believe it or not, I have always looked up to you." Martin was stunned by his brother's comment.

Though he was skeptical, it was a startling statement that caught Martin off-guard. "I don't hate you Matts, we're just different; that's all. We have gone our own ways." For a moment, Martin felt a wisp of shame. Why <u>did</u> he view his twin brother with such disdain? Was it jealousy? He didn't really know, but now he was eager to bring this uncomfortable conversation to an end.

"Why did you come here Matts?"

"You have a body in the morgue."

"I have several," Martin replied sarcastically.

Matts started again. "You have the body of one of our Venture Club members, Thomas Schmidt." Matts now looked up at his brother who was glaring fiercely into his eyes.

152

"Yes." His tone was as cold and sharp as an icicle.

"The sheriff told Arlo, er, one of our club members that you intend to do an autopsy on him."

"I am not sure how this is any of your business," Martin stated firmly, beginning to piece together the connection. He rocked back slowly in his chair.

Matts felt his way cautiously. "There is no reason for it. We all agree. Schmidt died of an unfortunate accident, brought on by excessive drinking. It's silly to make his family wait for a proper burial until you get around to doing something that's a waste of your valuable time, and the county's money."

The words came out in a mad rush. Matts had cycled the argument over and over in his head as he walked the several blocks from the Alford Building to St. Luke's, but his nerves had gotten the best of him.

Remembering Sheriff Chambers' remark about the threat made to Schmidt's life, Martin asked pointedly, "What are you afraid that I may discover?"

"Nothing. There is nothing to discover," Matts replied emphatically.

"Well if there _is_ nothing, you and your business associates have nothing to worry about, right?" Martin paused to let the words settle in. "_I_ believe the circumstances of this death are unclear, and it is my responsibility to investigate whether this was, as you insist, an accident, or something…else."

An uneasy silence returned, as Matts considered his next move. He did not want to report back to Arlo Peterson with bad news. Impulsively, he jumped to his feet and moved forward until his thighs rubbed up against the front of the doctor's desk. No longer thinking rationally, he summoned every ounce of courage and rage he could muster; his voice became surprisingly

153

loud and acrid as he waved his index finger in Martin's face.

"Damn you to hell. You've given me the bum's rush our entire lives, and I am sick of it. There will be <u>no</u> autopsy. You <u>will</u> release the body and issue a death certificate." Pausing for a moment he added, "If you decide to ignore this 'brotherly advice' you better keep your eyes open when you walk the streets at night."

His face was beet red until his moment of outrage flagged and his shoulders slumped. His arm dropped to his side. From the look on Martin's face, it appeared that he was clearly stunned and surprised by the outburst.

Martin was startled, and even a bit frightened by his brother's words and actions. Slowly he got to his feet and looked directly into the eyes of his brother. This man, his twin brother was a stranger; someone Martin could not, would not ever know. His earlier feeling of shame was now eclipsed by an impulse of rage as he tried to comprehend what was really going on. Was Matts trying to cover up for one of his business associates, or was he, a killer? Was it Matts who had threatened Thomas Schmidt? Martin could hardly believe that, but now, more than ever, the doctor knew an autopsy was needed to answer at least a few of these questions.

"We're done here," he said briskly. "And I am done with you. Leave and don't ever come here again."

Chapter 34

The lodge was now a brilliant orange torch tossing fireballs high into the night sky. Even though they were a good 75 yards away, continuous waves of heat washed over them. The sky reflected the orange light, making it likely that settlers as far away as Beaver Bay could see the glow. For a moment Martin was hypnotized by the ferocity of the blaze as it hungrily consumed the lodge. Stock slid next to Martin, his face occasionally illuminated by the fire. "Let's get 'em." he whispered earnestly, a severe, determined look on his face. Martin was stunned. As he was running from the incinerating lodge, he expected they would keep right on running. They had tunneled their way out of their log prison and the means of their escape was clear. Now Stock was suggesting that they turn and fight.

"Are you crazy, Ben? We need to get out of here while we can."

"Not on your life, Doc," Stock responded boldly. "Them bastards terrorized us, shot us, and tried to burn us up. I ain't leavin' til I get some answers and some vengeance. If you want to go, go, but I got unfinished business here."

In that moment, Andersen's body and mind convulsed with contending emotions. He too, wanted answers; why was his brother trying to kill him? After his long trek into the wilderness, the gunshots, the fire, he craved closure, or at least an explanation of why this was happening. But panic and his base instinct for survival told him that they needed to put their tails between their legs and run for their lives.

Now, in the flickering light from the slowly disappearing lodge, it was clear from the resolve plastered on Stock's face that he was spoiling for a fight. Martin decided he could not run now. They had been through a lot together in the last two days; he needed, they needed to see it through.

"What do you think we should do, Sarge?"

As always, Stock had been sketching out a plan in his mind. He wanted answers and revenge, but he knew it would be more difficult to get the former than the latter. "I'm guessin' one of them is hid out by each door, maybe 40-50 yards out or so. Close enough to get a good shot, but far enough away, so the fire ain't peeling their eyebrows off. Once they figure we're a pile of ashes, they'll probably relax some. One will come over to the other side to discuss what they should do. That's when we get the drop on them."

Martin thought it over. It sounded logical but again too risky for his liking. "But let's stick together, OK?" he spoke in a plaintive whisper. Ben had become his rock, his source of courage. Without him nearby, Martin was sure he could not within stand the strain and pressure. Stock nodded.

"Follow me, stay low, and be as quiet as you can."

The ferocious snapping and popping combined with the roar of gases being greedily consumed by the fire, drowned out the soft sounds they made as they circled around the lodge until they reached the shore of MicMac Lake. From there, they began sneaking in toward the lodge, slowly and cautiously. At a spot about 100 yards or so from the burning building, Stock stopped and nestled into a spot where he could peek through the thick layer of shrubs.

"This is good," he whispered as Andersen slid in next to Stock. Martin clung tightly to the shotgun, now surprised at how cold and foreign the barrel of the deadly weapon felt in his hands. After the roof had collapsed, the fire attacked the thick log walls. While the flames no longer shot as high in the sky, the heat was still intense. There could be no doubt that any living creature still in the building, be they man or insect, was now smoldering ash.

Several minutes later, Stock spotted movement to the right of the lodge. Whoever or whatever it was followed the fringe between light and dark heading in their direction. He tapped Andersen's thigh to alert him. A few tense minutes later, it was clear to both them that it was indeed one of their attackers. He was caring a gun, wearing a thick fur hat.

As they watched, the man wove his way around the building until he reached a point about halfway between the lodge and the spot where Stock and Andersen were hiding. The light of the burning lodge provided a powerful backlight, clearly defining his silhouette. In addition to the fur hat, he was wearing a ragged animal skin parka; a long stringy beard hung from his face.

As Stock and Andersen sat noiselessly, they watched as the man stopped and faint whispers could be heard. He was definitely talking to someone. Andersen tried make out what was being said, but could not. Stock leaned over placing his mouth next to Andersen's ear and whispered. "As soon as that other feller shows himself, we'll take 'em." Stock pointed to the right. "You slide over that way, and I'll go the other. Once they both appear, I'll call for 'em to drop their weapons;

157

when they do, we'll move in."

Most of the lodge was now lying in a glowing jackstraw heap. The flames were becoming blue, emitting less smoke as every drop of moisture was now dissipated. It was slowly becoming an enormous pile of white-hot coals. As Stock and Andersen carefully moved away from each other, Martin could feel fear returning. Though Ben was nearby, he was alone, again. He shivered, gripping the shotgun so tightly that his fingers began to ache. Once he reached a spot where he had a clear view of the man, he eased back the hammers on both barrels of the shotgun just as Stock had instructed.

After several minutes, the second attacker who had been sitting less than thirty yards or so from them, stood up. Adding his silhouette to the scene, he casually held the barrel of his rifle in this right hand, its stock resting on the ground. Andersen could now make out what they were saying.

"Well, that should take care of that. Nothing could have survived that bonfire."

"You'd think they'da made a run for it. Better to get shot then to burn to death, I'd say."

"Well, I guess. But job's done, let's get outta here and get our money."

Then out of the darkness, reverberating through the still cool night like the voice of God, Stock's booming command startled everyone and everything within earshot.

"Drop those guns, or you're dead men!"

The men wheeled around, trying to locate the source of the voice. Stock was well hidden, and after staring at the brilliant fire for so long the men's eyes were not adjusted to the deep shadows that lay beyond them. They saw nothing of Stock or Andersen.

158

"Drop 'em now," the voice growled again. This time, the threat had the desired effect and the men let their rifles fall to the ground. When they did, Stock rose to his feet, his head and torso slowly emerging from the thick bushes. With his rifle pinned tightly to his shoulder, the barrel leveled at the two men, Stock yelled, "Get yer hands in the air!" Slowly the men complied, as Ben stepped toward them, his rifle trained directly at them.

Then came that sound. It was high and mournful, clear and unwavering like the clarion call of a newly cast brass bell. Immediately, Andersen recognized it as the same sound he had heard echo through the woods two days earlier. Though difficult to locate, it seemed to be coming from the direction of Tettegouche Lake. To everyone who heard it that night, it was eerie and unnerving.

For just a brief moment, Stock's rifle wavered, momentarily distracted by the puzzling sound. It was not any sound an animal could make, he was certain of that. Seizing the opportunity provided by the distraction, the man with the long beard reached inside his jacket and pulled out a short-barreled revolver. Before Ben could react, the man fired, striking Ben in the side. As he was falling to the ground, Stock was able to get off one shot that sailed harmlessly past the head of the attacker.

Impulsively reacting with a seething concoction of rage and fear, Martin jumped to his feet, raised the shotgun to his shoulder and pulled both triggers at once. Inexperienced in how to properly hold a long gun, and totally unprepared for the fury of a double barreled blast of a 10 gauge shotgun, the thick walnut stock of the gun jolted backward into his chest and shoulder with such force that he was toppled backward to the ground; the

159

wind knocked from his lungs. As Martin lay stunned, trying desperately to regain his breath he heard a soft moan.

"Oh my God, Ben!"

Chapter 35

The St. Louis County morgue took up the entire east end of the basement level of St. Luke's Hospital. At Dr. Martin Andersen's urging, the county had recently provided funds to upgrade the morgue. Electric lights replaced the often shadowy gas lamps, and a larger number of more effective cold chambers were installed, cooled by blocks of Lake Superior ice.

Lying on a white porcelain steel table was the body of Thomas Schmidt. In reviewing his information before beginning the autopsy, Andersen learned that Schmidt was 45 years old, an American citizen who had come to this country in 1897, and was the managing partner of the Duluth and Northern Minnesota Railroad. There was no record of any health issues for which Schmidt had been treated.

As was standard protocol, Andersen began with a thorough external examination of the body. The anterior examination indicated nothing that could have contributed to a cause of death. There were several scars, long healed but no recent wounds, abrasions or bruising. Turning the body over, he continued the examination. At first, he again found little to indicate a possible cause of death. There were no wounds, cuts, or new marks of any kind. However, when he reached the cadaver's skull, Andersen detected a thick lump, that seemed larger then he would have expected from a normal variation of the human skull.

Parting the matted hair he could see a blotch of purple showing through the tightly packed follicles. With a scissors, and then a razor, he shaved the hair from the back of Schmidt's skull, finding a large oval contusion, thickly purple and puffy. Since blood collected there, he knew the wound was not post-mortem. He made careful drawings in his journal. Turning the body over, he now began to eviscerate the torso of the corpse. Cutting in a line from the armpit on each side of the victim to a meeting point directly below the sternum, he continued the incision through the abdomen down to the pubic bone. Once the cut was completed he methodically peeled back layers of skin and fat, revealing the rib cage and body cavity.

His main intent was to investigate whether the victim had, as everyone kept telling him, drowned. Victims of drowning usually had lungs filled with water, as in a last desperate, conditioned response, they breathe in the very water that will kill them. Those that die first and later end up in the water will generally have lungs free of water.

Accessing Schmidt's left lung, he made a long, deep incision starting as far up the organ as he could reach, and with practiced skill, continued down the inside of the lung and across the bottom. Before he had even finished the incision, water seeped from the lung into the body cavity.

'Well, they were partially right' Martin thought to himself.

Chapter 36

earing Ben's sorrowful moan spurred Martin to action; forgetting for the moment his badly bruised shoulder. Unsure, if the attackers were alive or dead, he feverishly dug into his jacket pocket, retrieving two of the shotgun shells Stock had given him as they fled the lodge. Fumbling in the dim light of the lodge's glowing remains, Andersen was finally able to open the breech of the shotgun, and extract the spent shells. He inserted fresh ones, and snapped the shotgun closed.

Slowly, he poked his head up, just far enough to see above the shrubs. Nothing was moving, and the only sound was the hushed wheezing coming from Ben's direction. Sinking back down below the shrubs he crawled the ten or so yards to where Ben was lying. Fearing the worst, Andersen was pleasantly astounded when Stock turned his head, and said with a touch of sarcasm, "I told you not ta' pull both triggers at once."

Taking Stock's comment as a good sign, he placed his mouth near to Stock's ear, whispering "where are you hit?"

"The bullet hit me in the side," Stock replied impatiently. "I been tryin' to hold my hand over the holes 'til you got here."

Andersen slipped the knapsack off Ben's back, and located his first aid kit. With Ben's help, he rolled him unto his left side, pulling back his buckskin jacket, and ratty shirt. In the faint light, he located the wounds. From what he could tell, Ben had been extremely lucky, if getting shot could ever be considered a stroke of good fortune. The bullet had pierced his side just above the hip bone and below the rib cage. It was what surgeons referred to as clean wound; with the bullet providentially avoiding bone and organ as it passed straight through the body. Martin splashed alcohol on the wounds, and then with Stock now sitting upright, managed to wrap a long bandage all the way around his waist.

As Martin worked, Ben began to interrogate him. "Did you get both them, Doc?"

"I don't know if I hit anything?" Andersen answered apologetically. "I was so scared, and then you got hit. I just stood and fired."

"Doc, I gotta believe you hit something. From that close range, there's enough lead flying around that even a mosquito would be lucky to survive." Stock took a deep, pain inducing breath. "And what, for God's sake ....what was that odd sound?"

Andersen had momentarily forgotten the ghostly sound that had echoed in the woods. "Was it an animal of some kind?"

"No animal I ever heard," Stock replied solemnly. "Sounded like a woman's voice to me."

With astounding strength and resilience, Stock rolled over, and got on his hands and knees. He slipped his knapsack on his back, and picked up this rifle. Quietly, he chambered another round, and waved for Andersen to follow him. Slowly, they crawled toward the smoldering lodge, to the spot where the two attackers had met their match, if not their maker. Stock stopped every few feet to listen for any sound that might provide a clue about the location of the two men. Finally, he stopped, turned back toward Martin and

164

whispered, "Well, you got one of 'em good."

Crawling up next to Stock, Dr. Martin Andersen, a man who had seen more than his share of human carnage, was physically sickened by what lay in front of him. The man with the long beard and fur hat lay flat on his back, his knees bent slightly upward, his arms splayed out like he was about to be nailed to a cross. The ferocious blast of a double load of buckshot had disemboweled him. His intestines oozed from his body, lying in bloody heaps next to him. His eyes were wide open, frozen in place from the quick and brutal extinguishment of his miserable life.

Dr. Andersen contemplated the actions of a medical man; someone dedicated to saving lives, now clearly responsible for taking one. How could it come to this, he wondered? What kind of man have I become? But, it was kill or be killed, Martin told himself; certainly logical and defensible, but much less soothing then he had hoped.

Stock moved past the dead man, searching the area for something else. "I think you winged the other bastard too."

"What?" Andersen was still trying to justify his feelings of remorse and relief; and now more death?

"He's bleeding, that's for sure."

Chapter 37

It was a delightfully warm Duluth evening as Dr.
Andersen walked the four blocks from St. Luke's to
the St. Louis County Jail. Constructed in 1889, the
sturdy two story red brick building featured brownstone
trim and carved stone accoutrements. The rear of the
building contained 16 jail cells where con men and
criminals of every stripe and national origin paid society
for their sins. Attached to the front of the jail, was a
house; the county-provided residence for the sheriff and
his family. In the name of efficiency, the sheriff's wife
was expected to prepare and serve meals to the prisoners
as part of the arrangement.

Climbing the steps to the small front porch, Dr.
Andersen knocked loudly on the heavy wood door. A
small boy, maybe six or seven years old with straight
black hair and a wide smile that revealed the absence of
his front teeth, greeted the doctor warmly.

"Hello mither. You lookin' for my pa?"

"Yes, I am son. Can you tell him that Dr.
Andersen is here to see him?"

Still standing in the doorway, the boy turned
around and yelled loudly, "Pa, a doctor ith here to see
ya."

"Let him in Isaac," came the familiar voice of
Willis Chambers, who now appeared in the doorway of
what was apparently the front parlor. Chambers brushed
back the thick mop of hair from his face, and motioned

166

for Martin to follow him. As they entered the parlor, seated on a green-dyed horsehair settee was a very distinguished looking man with steel gray hair parted straight down the middle of his head.

"Doc, have you met Mr. Peterson?" Chambers asked innocently. It was clear from Peterson's uncomfortable reaction that he was not that interested in meeting Dr. Andersen, at least not here in the Sheriff's home. Chambers seemed unconcerned.

With a perfunctory nod, Peterson acknowledged the doctor, and almost immediately pulled a finely engraved gold pocket watch from his vest. "Oh, got to be going Sheriff. I've got business to attend to." He stood to leave, carefully placing his hat on his head as he moved toward the door. Nodding at the doctor as he passed, he stared directly at Chambers. "Let me know what you find out," he said sternly and then he was gone.

"Please Doc, sit down," Chambers said graciously as he shooed an old tom cat from the settee; the cat having wasted little time reclaiming its favorite perch as soon as it was vacated.

Despite his brother's dire threat, and now maybe because of it, Martin was determined to follow through with the findings of the autopsy. As boys, Matts could often intimidate Martin with his bold, audacious attitude. But they were no longer boys, and Martin was intent on breaking out of the shackles of the past.

"Sheriff, I have completed the autopsy of Thomas Schmidt."

Chambers was surprised to hear that. He had hoped the coroner would seek the Sheriff's advice before proceeding, but Andersen had obviously taken it upon himself to conduct the medical procedure without his permission or knowledge, not that the law required that he do either of those things. Chambers now worried how he was going to explain what he was about to hear to Mr. Peterson. "I thought we agreed there weren't a need to do an autopsy," Chambers said with a disappointed tone.

Andersen shrugged his shoulders. Realizing that the deed had been done, he was now curious to find out what the Doctor had discovered. "So what *did* ya find out?"

"Well, in my opinion the actual cause of death *was* drowning. However, the deceased suffered a severe head trauma shortly before he drowned. My report will suggest that Mr. Schmidt was struck in the back of the head, and that once unconscious, he either fell, or was thrown into the water, where he drowned."

Chambers pursed his lips and exhaled a low whistle, as Martin continued. "I'm not going to tell you how to do your job, Sheriff, but I think you need to interrogate every member of the Venture Club and see if you can get a straight story from any of them."

"I understand there were some women there as well," the Sheriff replied, still trying to conjure up a story to tell his benefactor.

"Really?"

"Yes, you know, woman.....companions," Chambers offered tactfully.

In 1908, at the urging of several concerned citizens, the Duluth City Council decided that something must be done about the notorious 'Tenderloin District' that had taken root and blossomed along the waterfront of Duluth. For many years this concentration of 'evil resorts' as the newspapers labeled them, were well-known and well-supported by sailors, loggers, miners and residents alike. The city crackdown which included the temporary arrest of Madame Gain, the chief matron of Duluth's red light district, did little more than force Gain's premature retirement, and the hurried relocation of the 'houses of ill repute'. Four years later, the evil resorts were still as common as the corner speakeasies. And while some called for more aggressive police action, most, including the County Sheriff, found little value in trying to halt a trade so many sought comfort in.

"Do you know who they are, Sheriff?

"I only know one, her name is Sally somethin', she's a mick, got bright red hair."

"Well, I will send over the written report and death certificate tomorrow, Sheriff. I am willing to testify at trial when it gets to that point." With that Andersen stood up, shook the Sheriff's hand and headed toward the door. The boy, Isaac, was still trying to corral the spunky tom cat which now seemed determined to follow Martin out the door.

The evening sun had sunk behind the bluffs surrounding the city, casting the entire downtown into the shadows. Only the very top of the Alford Building stood high enough to capture the last direct rays of the sun, causing the top floor of the skyscraper to be bathed in an eerie reddish-orange glow. The soft breeze wafting in from the lake carried the strong odor of fish from the waterfront packing plants, and a touch of the residual chill from the cool lake water.

Martin shivered as he started down the hill, wishing now that he had thought to bring a jacket with him. The streets were quiet, with the occasional gas street lamp glowing along Superior St. As he approached St. Luke's he mentally tallied the patients he would need to check on before he could head home. There was the man who had been struck by an ice wagon suffering a compound fracture of his tibia; the workman who had fallen from scaffolding in one of the waterfront warehouses breaking several ribs, and the red-haired woman, Sally.....suddenly it struck him like a streetcar careening downhill. Sally, Sally Keefe, the Irish woman with the bright red hair. It had to be. Her head wound, her mistaking him for his brother, the fear in her eyes; it was all starting to make sense.

Chapter 38

Though Stock was eager to follow the blood trail he knew would lead them to the remaining attacker, darkness and the element of surprise favored their quarry. They would have to wait for daylight, Stock informed Martin.

Cold, exhausted and hungry, they crept closer to the steaming pile of embers to soak up as much of the residual heat as they could. Finding a spot that provided thick cover, yet close enough to stay warm, they lay quietly on the ground. As the adrenaline subsided in his body, Stock felt the return of the sharp pain in his left arm and now his pulsating right side. Sitting stiffly on the soft cold ground, Stock wished he had thought to bring some vittles from his larder. His stomach growled and ached, adding one more stream of pain to his tortured body. "Get some sleep" he had encouraged Martin. "I can't sleep anyway."

After several restless hours, high thin clouds in the eastern sky began to glow red and yellow as the spin of the earth brought the sun closer to the horizon. Martin had been able to catch a bit of sleep; Stock, none at all. He felt as if he had been run over by an angry bull, with pain shooting down his arm and up from his hip. Yet, all night, he had been formulating another plan, a sockdolager that would bring this nightmare to an end. Now as the sun eased above the horizon, he was ready to make his move.

He slid over to where Dr. Andersen was lying, and related his plan. He would take the point, following what he hoped would be a traceable trail of blood until they came upon or spooked their game. Ben directed Martin to stay five yards off to the left and slightly behind. "We don't want to bunch up, and give that varmint a chance to pot both of us." Stock spoke as casually as if he were discussing the weather. Andersen, again struggling to find his courage was still convinced they should skedaddle while they were still breathing. But placing his trust, and life, in Stock's hands, they set off, together.

Crawling and slithering forward, Stock had the look of a mangy bloodhound on the scent as he moved slowly and confidently. Off to his left, Andersen mirrored Ben's moves, staying low, and staring through the tightly packed stems of the underbrush for any movement, shadow or color, that did not belong. As Stock picked up the trail, he discovered that the blood spots were small, thin and widely spaced; not heavy and continuous as he had hoped. 'Not wounded too bad' he thought to himself. And for a brief second, Ben worried that their prey might now be a county away.

The blood trail was leading them down the slope toward Tettegouche Lake. Stock considered this a good sign. During his time on the western front, he had seen badly wounded men crying out for a cool drink of water, above anything else. Slowly now, with eyes and eyes keenly focused, they continued to crawl down the slope toward the lake.

Though the near shore was still cast in shadows, the main body of the lake shimmered, as a soft puff of wind stirred up the surface just enough to reflect the morning sun's rays. Heavy drops of dew hung from the

172

few remaining leaves on the trees and dense underbrush, adding a sparkling glow to the forest. It looked so peaceful and beautiful; it was difficult to accept that death was likely lurking just up ahead.

Stock and Andersen were about halfway down the slope toward the lake, when Ben unexpectedly stopped moving. Andersen froze in place, hoping that Stock had located their attacker, dead or dying. A few moments later, Ben popped out of the thick brush, his face covered in sweat and a long look of disappointment. "The trail's run out," he reported with obvious disappointment.

Martin needed little encouragement to forsake their mission, and decided that now was the time to throw in their cards. "Let's get out of here Ben," he whispered. "We could be heading straight into an ambush."

Ben shook his head. "We're gonna end this," he said with defiance, "right here!"

Martin realized he was shaking again, veiled in a cloak of fear as powerful as that one which had struck him that very first night in the lodge. Every cell of his body, urged him to make a run for it. One dead man was enough. No amount of insight on why this was happening was worth the grizzly end Martin feared was waiting for them down by the lake's edge. Yet Stock was not to be deterred.

Putting his mouth so close to Martin's ear that he could feel and hear his soft breathe, he whispered, "I'm dang sure he is down by the lake. Let's split up, and flank him; you head off to the left, and I will head off to the right. Move slow, stay low, and stop ever' so often to listen."

Martin nodded, taming his better instincts to flee. With a nod toward Stock, which Martin now feared

173

might be the last time they would see each other alive, they split up and began to find their separate ways down to the lake. As Martin crawled, he gripped the heavy shotgun in his right hand, at times using it to push through the thick brush. At Stock's direction, he had not cocked the hammers for fear the brush might grab one of the triggers and set off a blast.

And then came that sound. Just as it did the previous night, the high, melodic tone interrupted the softly singing birds, flaunting the quiet of the morning air. It lasted for five seconds or so; a haunting sound that echoed deep into the thick forest. From where Martin was laying, it seemed to come directly from chilly depths of Tettegouche Lake.

Urged on by a force he could not see or comprehend; suddenly unencumbered by fear or doubt, he jumped to his feet, cocking both hammers of the shotgun as he did. Standing in the dappled morning sunlight, Martin spotted the man dressed in a dirty buckskin jacket and beaver pelt hat just twenty yards away, staring down the sights of a rifle trained on a spot just in front of him. In the next instant, the sounds of mayhem and death drowned out the siren call and everything else within earshot.

Martin held the stock of the shotgun tightly to his shoulder, and this time with clear intent, unleashed both barrels at the man while screaming "Ben look out!"At that same instant, the man in tattered buckskin fired his gun toward the ground in front of him.

Though more prepared for the recoil this time, Martin was still rocked backward by the powerful explosion of two 10 gauge shotgun shells. This time, a thick clump of young birch trees halted his fall, catching him in its soft branches. Though he remained standing, he was struck with an attack of the jelly legs as he witnessed the damage he had wrought upon the remaining attacker.

It was as if the man's body exploded. Chunks of flesh and bone, and a misty curtain of blood erupted into the air, forming a sheen that reflected bright red in the gathering sunlight. What remained of the broken body fell to the ground like a sack of onions, as his long gun flew over his head and landed behind the bloody heap. The sight of what he had done made Martin sick to his stomach.

After a few pained seconds, Andersen gathered his wits, dropped the empty shotgun and ran to where he thought Stock was lying. The eerie sound that had alerted him to the attacker's presence haunted his thoughts as he scrambled down the slope. 'What was it?' he wondered.

A moment later he stumbled upon Stock, who was lying face down, his arms splayed out to either side, his trusty Winchester lying just beyond the reach of his right arm. There was a splotch of blood visible on the back of his head. As best he could tell, Stock was dead.

Chapter 39

octor Andersen entered the woman's convalescent area at St. Luke's. The room, located on the second floor, was painted stark white; the floor covered with plain white tile. Ten beds, placed in two groups of five were positioned on either side of the water closet. Each bed was encircled with heavy cloth drapes. Large, cast iron sinks, coated in white enamel, hung from the wall on each end of the long, narrow room; a small mirror positioned above each.

The water closet which featured a newly installed flush toilet was positioned between the two sets of five beds. A large zinc water tank was elevated high above the toilet and was proudly embossed with the trademark 'Crapper's Valveless Waste Preventer.' Andersen checked the assignment chart, and found that Sally was in bed number seven. As he approached her bed, he saw that the drape was open; Andersen walked in.

"How are you feeling Sally? he asked gently.

Her face had been scrubbed, her hair washed and combed. What had appeared as a bedraggled street urchin a day earlier, was now a lovely, attractive woman. Her eyes followed Martin intently as he entered. Despite his earlier explanation that he and Matts were identical twins, his appearance still startled her.

"A little better," she offered cautiously.

"Miss Keefe, can you tell me about your injury; how did it happen?"

Since leaving Grand Rapids, Sally Keefe made her way in the world trusting few people. Though she now realized the doctor was trying to help her, she could not be certain that his brotherly connection to the Venture Club would not be the source of more injury or attacks. She proceeded warily.

"I don't really know."

Andersen decided to lay one of his cards on the table, "Did someone attack you at Tettegouche Camp?" Sally bolted straight up in her bed, staring at the doctor in disbelief.

"How did you know about that?"

Calmly, Martin sat down on the edge of her bed, his face now close to Sally's. Her jade green eyes glowed in the bright lights of the room, and inexplicably, he felt very close to her. "I know that some bad things happened up there. A man died under..... unusual circumstances." Andersen parsed his words carefully.

Swept up by suddenly unwieldy emotions, Sally cried "they killed Hannah too," as she buried her face in Andersen's shoulder. Spontaneously, he hugged her tightly; feeling empathy, sadness and a human stirring that due to his single-minded pursuit of his career, had been absent from his life. Catching herself, she tried to push away from Martin as a stream of tears rolled down her cheeks. Martin clung to her tenderly. "Sally, what are you talking about?"

"Hannah, one of the girls, she saw the murder. She didn't know who it was for sure. But she saw the murder. Well, whoever killed Mr. Schmidt must have figured that out, and knew she needed to be silenced. I was trying to help her escape when I was attacked."

"We need to tell this story to Sheriff Chambers, Sally."

"Not if I want to live through this day," Sally fired back. "Everyone in town knows that Chambers is Arlo Peterson's man. If I tell them what I know, they will see me dead."

Dr. Andersen was taken aback. Could Sally be right about this? Are respected business and community leaders murdering innocent people to protect.....to protect what?

"As soon as you let me outta here, I'm takin'the next train south."

Chapter 40

"Sarge...Ben, can you hear me?" Stock's body was motionless, except for a barely perceptible movement of his torso, indicating that he was still breathing, still alive. Andersen dropped to his knees, and examined the wound on the back of his head. Pulling back the dirty, matted hair, Martin could see blood seeping from the wound. It appeared the bullet did not pierce the skull, rather plowed a rough deep furrow through the scalp and skull. Stock was clearly unconscious, not surprising given the sledge hammer blow delivered by the heavy rifled slug burrowing through his head.

Removing the nearly depleted first aid kit from Ben's knapsack, he dabbed the last of the alcohol on the wound, trying to clean it as best he could before tightly wrapping a bandage around his head. Once that was completed, he gently rolled Stock onto his back, propping his canvas jacket under Stock's neck.

Stock's breathing was erratic and shallow. His pulse was rapid, and so weak that Martin could barely feel it on his wrist or neck. While certain that Stock could not hear him, Martin found it necessary to share with Ben his ominous diagnosis.

"Ben, I fear you are in a bad way. I have done what I can, but in this wilderness that's not much, possibly not enough." Martin tenderly ran the back of his hand across Stock's forehead. The skin was cold, too cold.

"You have been a better friend to me than I deserve, probably the best friend I've ever had." Tears began to fill his eyes, and he trembled uncontrollably as he watched Stock labor to breathe. "I can never repay you for what you have done for me. Without you, I would have been dead, several times over. I am <u>so</u> sorry for the pain and suffering I have caused you." Martin stopped and took a deep breath.

"Two nights ago, you asked me why I had come to the Camp. I told you it was because of the letter from my brother. Well, that was just part of the reason, Ben. I came here to confront my brother, to confront my fears, to force him to tell me the truth about what happened here and back in Duluth. For years I have been afraid, afraid to stand up to him, afraid to do the right thing."

Ben Stock, the old soldier, was tough as nails, but as Doctor Andersen suspected, sepsis, a poisoning of the blood brought on by his several gunshot wounds, was now systematically shutting down his organs. There was nothing that any doctor could do now.

"Ben, this is not over. I will find out who is responsible for this, and bring them to justice. This I promise you." Martin gently held Ben's hand, which was rough and cold. And then from the direction of Tettegouche Lake, the same mysterious melodic sound once again echoed through the still morning air. Clear and plaintive, eerie and forlorn, it again sent shivers down Martin's spine. It disappeared as suddenly as it came. It was then that Sergeant Benjamin Stock took his last breath.

Martin was not a man of god; did not hold fast to the notion of an afterlife. Yet he now felt compelled to offer a brief prayer over the body. Placing his hand on Stock's shoulder, with his eyes turned skyward, he said

180

"Please take this good man, protect him and lead him to the place of honor he deserves."

With prayers offered, it was now Martin's duty to provide Stock a proper burial. Lacking a shovel and confronted by thin rocky ground, it was clear that digging a hole would be nearly impossible. He decided that a rock cairn was the best he could do. Locating a slight rise overlooking Tettegouche Lake, he muscled Stock's heavy body down a short incline to his final resting spot. Removing the holster from around Stock's waist, and the knapsack from his back, he folded Ben's arms in front on him, and began the sorrowful task of encasing the body in rock and stone.

While consumed by his mournful obligation, Martin took little notice that the bright mid-day sun was slowly disappearing behind an inky curtain of ominous-looking clouds. The warm breeze that had flowed in from the south much of the morning had slackened, and was beginning to evolve into a brisk wind pushing in from the northwest.

In northeastern Minnesota, late fall can be as unpredictable as a newly broke stallion. Occasionally, persistent breezes roll in from the southwest pushing pleasant pools of warm, moist air into the region. And while roving bands of Ojibwe and early settlers grew to appreciate this brief reprieve from a looming winter, they also understood it was a game of three card monte; a con for the unsuspecting.

For the whirling vortex that was yanking warm air in from the south, would soon begin to inhale frigid Canadian air in from the north, creating a head-on collision between competing air masses. The brutish results were heavy bursts of wet snow whipped to a froth by bone-chilling arctic winds forming blizzard conditions fully capable of punishing the unknowing or unprepared. Fueled by limitless amounts of moisture provided by an unfrozen Lake Superior, snow could pile up fast and deep; two to three feet was always possible.

It wasn't until Martin had finished placing the final stones around and over Stock's body that he noticed the darkening sky, and felt the chill wind. From his years in Duluth he suspected what was about to happen and knew that time was now his foe. After completing the cairn, he rushed to search out the remains of their attackers.

The body of the man most recently killed was still warm, though the blood had coagulated. His eyes were wide open, his face frozen in a last futile look of determination. Martin searched the man's pockets for any oddments that could provide a clue as to who had hired the scoundrels for such dirty work. Other than a couple plugs of chewing tobacco and a small pocket knife, he found nothing of substance.

Locating the broken body of the other man, the one with the long, stringy beard, Andersen discovered that he had a small satchel strapped to his side. Lifeless for half a day, the body was stiff as a board; the exposed intestines and organs had turned a shiny dark brick red. In the satchel, he discovered some jerky, several apples, and then, what he was hoping to find.

It was an envelope containing a cryptic note and a stack of crisp greenbacks that totaled $200. The note described the job to be done, and that $400 more dollars would be earned once the task was completed. At the bottom were initials, likely those of the man who had written the note. A look of surprise followed by a mask of fury enveloped Martin's face.

"I've got to get back to Duluth," he bellowed into the gathering storm.

Chapter 41

Sheriff Chambers slowly opened the large white envelope that he found placed neatly in the middle of his desk. It was embossed with St. Luke's Hospital imprimatur. He ripped open the seal, and pulled out the now familiar autopsy report form. Along with the basic report were hand rendered drawings of the anterior and posterior sides of the corpse of Mr. Thomas Schmidt.

As Dr. Andersen had informed the Sheriff the day before, his written conclusion was that the deceased had died from drowning, but that a blunt force injury to the head most likely caused the drowning to occur.

Chambers sat for a moment, perplexed. As a lawman he knew that together with the threat that Schmidt had reported, the findings of the autopsy were sufficient to consider this a possible homicide, or at least enough to open an investigation. But as a man who owed his job and future to Arlo Peterson, he was certain that such a move could jeopardize both. He felt as if his bollocks were in a vice.

Corralling his long black hair and stuffing it in his uniform hat, he headed for the door of the office. "Sophia, I am going down to St. Luke's," Chambers called out to the young office girl whose job it was, in part, to keep track of the Sheriff's whereabouts.

"When will you be back?" she asked cheerily.

"Shortly," Chambers replied with an uncharacteristically sharp tone. He was not looking forward to what he was about to do. But his only other choice was one he disliked even more. Hoping to catch the doctor in his office, Chambers took the back stairway up to the third floor of the hospital. He saw that Andersen's door was open, the electric lights switched on. Martin, it seemed, was not at all surprised at the sudden appearance of the Sheriff at his office door and had a pretty good idea of what the Sheriff was going to say.

"Evenin' Doc. Can I come in?"

Andersen nodded and pointed toward the chair in front of his desk. He removed his reading spectacles, laid them deliberately on his desk and folded his arms in front of him. Already suspecting the answer, Dr. Andersen asked quietly, "Have you read the autopsy report?"

"Yes, Chambers responded as he flopped down in the chair."

"And?"

Chambers was clearly uncomfortable as he fidgeted like a rambunctious two year old in church, while wringing the life from his tortured cap. He cleared his throat and wiped his mouth on the back of the sleeve. "Doc, appears to me there just ain't enough evidence to open an investigation."

Andersen was not surprised, but still angered at what he considered a lack of professional conduct by the Sheriff. "Did you interview *any* of the men of the Venture Club?" Andersen asked pointedly.

"Well, I talked to Arlo...Arlo Peterson; asked him what happened. He told me the whole story...seems it was clearly an accident, nothing more."

"Do you know who found the body?"

"It was Peterson."

"How deep was the water where the body was found?" Andersen had now taken on the mantle of an

184

investigator, digging into the facts to discern the truth.

At first, Chambers was puzzled by the question, until it occurred to him that this was an important piece of evidence. "I, I don't know for sure......Peterson said he waded 10 yards or so out into the lake to identify him."

"So an able-bodied adult man drowns in a couple feet of water, 30 feet from the shore?" Andersen asked rhetorically, his voice dripping with sarcasm.

"He was drunk....probably just passed out." Chambers countered, getting more defensive as he realized he was now making up his own facts, and excuses.

"What about the head wound? That was a severe injury!"

Chambers stopped torturing his hat and looked directly at the coroner. Though Chambers was slow to get his dander up, he could feel his cheeks warming, his heart pounding faster. "Listen, I got the only story, I'm gonna get. None of them men is going to tell me anything different than what Peterson told me. So unless you got an eye witness that swears on the Holy Bible to a different story, there ain't no case to open."

Andersen shot to his feet, prepared to launch into a bitter tirade, accusing the Sheriff of cowardice, failing to do his sworn duty, laziness. But once on his feet, he realized that there was really nothing more he was prepared to do. He was afraid to cross swords with the county sheriff who could make trouble for Martin. The Sheriff's mind was clearly made up, or had it made up for him, and no amount of jawboning was going to change that.

Dejectedly, Andersen stared down at his hands. "Alright Willis, my instinct tells me that a killer is getting away with murder, but the blood is on your hands."

Chambers got to his feet, hesitated for a moment as he considered saying something more, then turned and skulked out of Andersen's office. He hoped that this was the end of it; that things would now settle down.

Unfortunately, it would only take a few days before he would discover that this was not over, not by a long shot.

Chapter 42

The first snowflakes to leak from the leaden clouds now hovering over the remains of the Tettegouche lodge were as soft and fluffy as goose down. They fluttered slowly and peacefully from the sky attaching themselves to the rocks and trees. Though the bucolic conditions would never suggest it, Martin realized he was about to face a life or death decision.

He could hole up in one of the rundown bunkhouses, out of the snow and wind until the storm passed. But slogging ten miles through waist-deep snow without snowshoes or food, and pitifully inadequate clothing was at best, a fool's errand.

He could head toward the Village of Lax Lake. It was much closer then the way he came, and it was possible that the original access road from Lax Lake to the camp might still be discernible. But he was totally unfamiliar with that area and would need to head northwest, directly into the teeth of the storm. And if the trail ran out, which was entirely possible, he could miss the tiny village completely and end up wandering into the deepest and most remote areas in all of Minnesota.

The final option was to try to outrace the storm by making a mad dash for Beaver Bay. Though the heavy clouds filled with a ready blanket of snow were turning daylight into twilight, Andersen figured he had about five hours before blackness closed in. And while his compass was now a pool of melted brass somewhere in the ashes of the lodge, he was confident that the howling northwest wind would provide a steady guide; 'if I keep the wind to my back' he thought with a tinge of gallows humor, 'it will be pretty hard for me to miss Lake Superior.'

Making up his mind, one filled with hope, anger and unexpected determination, he snugged up Stock's knapsack still containing the thick envelope of legal papers, and added the hand written note and money taken from the attacker. To keep his load light, he would take only his pistol; which forced him, sadly, to abandon the shotgun and rifle. He felt a sense of painful remorse in not protecting Mr. Stock's most prized possessions.

As he was about to head out, he suddenly remembered that the attacker with the long beard had several sticks of jerky and apples in his satchel, which Andersen now retrieved and placed in his knapsack. As he did, he eyed the man's thick fur hat, realizing that whatever clothing he could secure might make a difference. With some distain he snatched the ratty looking hat from the man's head, and shook it vigorously several times before pulling it firmly down over his ears. It smelled like skunk. Setting his bearings from the layout of the camp and the direction of the wind, he set out.

For the first hour, the going was good. Though the forest was as dense and unforgiving as before, he made good time. With only a coating of snow, and the wind to his back, he felt warm…and hopeful. Soon, however, the swirling wind began to churn fresh Canadian cold into the moisture laden air from the lake. Snowflakes that were as soft as bed pillows now grew hard and biting; creating a dense screen of white that began to close in around him.

During the second hour, travel became more treacherous as the rocks and slopes became slippery with snow and ice. Several times, Andersen fell to his knees as his feet shot out from under him. Undaunted, he would pop up, brush himself off, and keep moving. Due to the heavy exertion of his pace, his body continued to stay comfortably warm. However, his thin leather boots provided little warmth, and he soon noticed that his toes were starting to tingle. First signs of frostbite, he thought to himself. During his years at St. Luke's he had treated a number of patients with fingers or toes, ears and noses as black as coal. Gangrene allowed for only one remedy which began with a heavy dose of ether and ended with a sharp scalpel or bone saw.

By mid-afternoon, the fury of the wind began buffeting him, and pushing the heavily falling snow with brutal authority. At times, the snow came horizontally, creating a supernatural feel to the woods around him. Then, without warning a flash of light pierced the steel-grey sky. Mystified, Martin looked up, wondering if he was imagining things. Then a powerful clap of thunder rolled across the stark white landscape shaking the ground, the trees, and for some moments, Martin's nerve. Known to the Ojibwe as *animikii-goon*, or thunder snow, it was an ominous and undeniable signal from the heavens that this snowstorm was about to become even more ferocious.

He pulled the skunk hat down on his head as far as it would go, sticking the collar of his canvas coat underneath to keep the snow from sliding down his back. Nearly six inches of snow now blanketed the ground, forcing him to step higher and more cautiously to avoid tripping and falling.

Another hour passed, and now nearing exhaustion, Martin looked for any sort of refuge to take a needed break. Up ahead, a large white spruce loomed in his path. Gratefully he crawled under its dense, protective limbs, which provided welcome relief from the snow and the wind. He burrowed in close to the trunk of the enormous tree so he could prop his back against it. He ravenously pulled a piece of jerky and one of the apples from his knapsack. As he devoured the food, he cowered under the tight canopy of limbs.

Staring out into the blinding landscape, he felt utterly alone; more alone than he ever thought possible. It was if he was the only human being on the earth. There was no sound but the wind, rushing and whistling through the creaking branches of the brittle trees. Not a creature was moving through the torrents of snow. Peering out from his bright white cocoon, he began to wonder whether he had made a fatal mistake. Maybe he should have waited the storm out. It would have likely passed in a day or two, and though he would have had to contend with waist-high snow drifts, he likely would have the sun to guide him.

Then, suddenly, above his head, the accumulated load of snow overcame the heavily laden spruce limbs, and an avalanche cascaded down and through the tree, layering him with snow. Andersen was startled, and yet reminded that questioning his decision now, would bring him no closer to safety. He had made his choice. He would live with it; or die because of it.

His body was now cool, and perspiration was becoming another enemy. He shivered uncontrollably. He had to get moving, now. Crawling out from under the thick limbs of the spruce, Martin straightened up his knapsack, turned until the wind struck him directly in the back and headed into the foaming maelstrom. The snow was nearly to his knees now, so each step became more strenuous and tiring than the last. He walked hunched over, keeping his head down; peering up only occasionally to locate the easiest path through the forest. As he plodded on, he discovered that his toes no longer ached, a dangerous sign. His feet were starting to feel like blocks of ice. Stopping only occasionally to catch his breath, he would quickly start again, realizing that every minute of delay would add another layer of snow to the fast rising drifts.

It was late afternoon, he estimated, when he stopped again under another hospitable spruce. He inhaled the last of his meager provisions, washing them down with several handfuls of snow. If he was right, he would have another hour or so of muted daylight before the forest would become as dark and impenetrable as a coal mine. He wondered if he should try to start a fire, to warm his frozen feet and wait out the storm until morning. Again he decided that his best choice was to keep moving, keep pushing.

Sliding out from under the drooping branches of the spruce, Martin again plowed resolutely into a colorless landscape; the negligible contrast between white and grey in the dimming light provided little definition of what was ahead in the windswept forest. Blasts of snow-filled wind pushed him along, before swirling around him in several directions.

The snow was now so deep that walking became treacherous. As exhaustion and cold seemed to incase his legs in lead, buried rocks and tree limbs became unseen and unforgiving obstacles. With alarming frequency he would slip and fall. With each step and each fall, he could feel the energy being sucked from his body. But still he pushed onward. After another half hour or so, fear began to seize his slowly dissolving spirit. He started to believe that he wasn't going to make it; that his unlikely journey to Tettegouche Camp would be his last worldly act. From the moment he left Duluth, heading for Beaver Bay, he tortured himself with the simple question of "Why?" Now, as the snow swirled around him, he began to doubt that he would ever get a chance to answer that question.

Chapter 43

The body of Thomas Schmidt was laid to rest in the shadow of an impressive Italian marble headstone in Forest Hills Cemetery. Unlike Duluth's Park Hill Cemetery, Forest Hills was intended for the rich and powerful. So as Schmidt had hoped to achieve in life, it was only in death that he found himself accepted into the company of Duluth's most wealthy and prominent; who ultimately discovered, as he did, that money and influence proved woefully inadequate in forestalling the grim reaper.

Alan Prescott, John Wentworth, Matts Andersen, Billy O'Leary and Arlo Peterson stood together in the cool shade of the bur oak and jack pine that clung to the rocky hillside overlooking east Duluth. Missing from the group, Anders Johnson had let Peterson know that he would not be coming to the service, and had no intention of being part of the Duluth Venture Club from this point forward.

It was a tiny gathering of mourners, as Schmidt had few blood relations in the area, and fewer friends. Several business associates and a few curious locals stood near the casket as it hung poised over the empty, expectant hole in the rocky ground. A Lutheran minister quietly uttered verses of scripture and a few solemn words intended to faithfully usher the spirit of the deceased into the afterlife.

Growing impatient, Prescott pulled his watch from the breast pocket of this black silk vest. He was eager to get back to the office. With no heirs to contend with, Prescott now assumed he was the sole owner of the D&NM railroad. He had some ideas on how things would change and was eager to get started. Wentworth took notice of Prescott's restlessness, tapped him on the elbow, and with a slight twitch of the head, motioned Prescott to join him under the sweeping boughs of a nearby oak tree.

"This isn't over quite yet," Wentworth whispered to Prescott. Prescott stared at the young attorney, a look of confusion on his face.

"What do you mean?"

"Schmidt filed a revised will the day before he left for the Camp."

"What?" Prescott's voice thundered across the cemetery. Several of the 'aggrieved' mourners turned and stared at the two men. Prescott caught himself, and lowered his voice.

"How did this happen?"

"Schmidt had another attorney prepare and file the will with the clerk of court," Wentworth explained.

"How do you know this?" Prescott was beginning to see his carefully laid plans dissolving before his eyes.

"The attorney presented the will in probate court this morning. The judge took it under advisement and will decide in several days, which of the wills he will honor." Wentworth slowly shook his head, clearly feigning empathy.

Prescott was visibly shaken, unsure what to do next. The minister had finished the brief service, and the two grimy grave diggers, who had been leaning casually on their shovels nearby, stepped forward, ready to fulfill their role in the inevitable circle of life.

As Prescott and Wentworth made their way back across the monument strewn hillside, they could hear Peterson speaking in a low voice. "Well, that's the end of that," he said vacantly, staring out across the cemetery grounds. However, Billy O'Leary was not so quick to move on. His gut was churning with disgust, now more than ever; certain that Prescott had gotten away with murder.

As Scottie and Wentworth drew near, O'Leary accosted him. "So ya now have the railroads all to ya self," he said sarcastically, staring daggers at Prescott.

Always ready to have a go at it, Prescott shot back, "Watch yourself O'Leary. You never know when you might end up going for a swim." Peterson stepped between the two men, and placed his hands on their shoulders trying to once again tamp down the sputtering fuse between them.

"This is over. There is nothing that can be done now. Let's go down to Fitgers and drink a toast to our dear friend departed."

O'Leary shook his head. "I'm done with this," he replied cryptically. Though he didn't want to cross his mentor, he could no longer abide by the fact that a murderer among them was walking away a free man. "I'm going back to my office." He turned on his heel and took off down the hill as the other men silently boarded their carriages, and headed toward one of Duluth most notable saloons.

While the passing of Schmidt was being memorialized, Dr. Martin Andersen was in the midst of another endless day filled with a gauntlet of sick, injured and dead at St. Luke's Hospital. Working without a break from early morning, the sun had nearly disappeared behind the bluffs above Duluth, before Dr.

195

Andersen found a minute to rest.

Throughout the long day, while his skilled hands cut and patched a stream of patients both living and dead, his every thought was consumed by Sally. It was her raw beauty, for sure. And her steely temperament as well, yet he struggled to comprehend and accept his unexpectedly torrid feelings toward her; feelings that were deeper and more complex than he had felt for any woman. And though he knew nothing of her past, other than she survived by selling her companionship to others, Martin was drawn to her, like the proverbial moth to a flame. Martin now realized that while it was crystal clear that Sally was rock hard on the outside, she was indeed a sad and lonesome waif; someone scraping through life depending on her wits and determination to protect her.

As his workday ended, Andersen quickly made his way to the women's convalescent ward. The drape was drawn around Sally's bed, and he politely announced his presence as he slid back the heavy curtain. Surprisingly, Sally was sitting on the edge of her bed, fully dressed, laboring to fasten her high-button boots.

"Where do you think you are going, Miss Keefe?" Martin stated firmly.

"I'm takin' meself home," she replied with a defiance equally as firm.

"I have not yet released you from hospital care," Martin countered with a professional tone.

"I'm leaving, and that's the end of it." Her jaw was set and her jade colored eyes blazed with resolve.

Andersen instantly knew that any more attempts to cajole her into staying were useless. Sally was a determined soul and her mind was clearly made up. "Then please, let me walk you home, Sally," he said softly. "You are still unsteady from your injury, and I want to make sure you get there safely."

Sally gazed up at the doctor for a moment. Her nature of self-reliance was being challenged by a sense of dread and danger she feared lurked outside the safety of the hospital. After offering a plaintive, half-hearted objection, she nodded. Standing up, she fastened a shiny green hat atop her mound of curly red hair with a large hatpin as Andersen retrieved her grip. Together, they made their way slowly down the stairs, out the side door of the hospital, and up the hill toward Sally's boarding room.

Though she had felt strong and rested as they started out, lying in a hospital bed for several days had sapped her strength more than she could imagine. As they ascended the steep hill, she looped her arm through Martin's. Drawing strength and balance from his sturdy arm, she felt safe, for likely the first time in her life; bathed in a feeling of serenity emanating from the doctor's caring nature. Almost as one, they traversed the several city blocks to her room. No words were said; none were needed. Arriving at the front door of the modest wood-frame boarding house, Sally stopped and looked up into the soft blue eyes of the doctor, hesitating, searching for the right words to say.

"I live on the second floor," she said with a child-like tone to her voice. "I would be appreciatin' a hand up the stairs."

Andersen nodded eagerly as he tenderly clasped Sally's arm with one hand, and her suitcase with the other. The front stairwell was dark, and the well worn steps creaked eerily as they slowly climbed the two flights together. A dark narrow hallway, faintly lit with a single kerosene lamp, greeted them as they reached the second floor.

"The door to me flat is second on the left," Sally announced and she handed Martin a large brass key which she produced from the pocket of her dress.

Her room was tiny; dark and ghostly as a cave. A single window partially covered with a stained and tattered roller shade provided a hint of light. The boarding house was just outside the reach of the city's new electrical grid, where thick strands of black wire drooped from tall poles along the major thoroughfares of downtown Duluth. So after placing her grip on the floor and helping Sally settle into the one plain pine chair, Martin lit several wall-mounted kerosene lamps. The room brightened; revealing Sally's modest world.

Along the far wall, a weathered wash stand with a white porcelain pitcher and bowl stood next to a tall pine armoire. A small metal frame bed was pushed up against one wall, a blackened coal-burning heater sat near nearby. There was a single dusty unframed picture of several people stuck to the wall above a tiny cook stove. Several green painted cabinets and a small cast iron sink took up residence along the opposite wall.

Seeing there was just one chair, Martin sat gingerly on the foot of the bed. For a moment there was an uncomfortable silence, as each wondered what the other was thinking. Martin finally found his voice, falling back on his role as doctor.

"Sally, how are you feeling now?" Martin spoke with a kindness and concern that was foreign to the young woman.

"I'm feelin' a bit punk, but no worse for the wear, I reckon." Her normally alabaster cheeks were red as spring roses, causing her bright green eyes to shine with even more effervescence than usual. As he stared into the shimmering pools of green, he felt as if he was

198

about to swallowed up.

Then like a bolt from the heavens, Sally said "Doctor Andersen, can...can I call you Martin?"

"Of course," he said, his head bobbing like a marionette.

"I am scared Martin. The man who attacked me knows where I live, and he will come again for me." She reached out her arm, and gently folded her tiny hand into Martin's. "Please....would you....stay with me tonight?"

Without hesitation, Martin slid from the bed and on his knees cradled Sally in a tender embrace as she leaned forward and wrapped her arms around Martin. The warmth of each others' bodies flooded over them, and soon their lips met in a tender, passionate kiss.

"I am here Sally, don't worry."

Chapter 44

A crusty layer of ice hung from his goatee, as the whirling vortex of snow continued. Martin realized that he could go no further. Snow now covered the ground above his knees. He could no longer feel his fingers and toes. With each painful step, geysers of frosted breathe erupted from his mouth as his lungs burned, laboring fitfully to keep him moving. He had reached the end of his endurance. Searching the ivory landscape for any sort of refuge, he spotted a tight clump of white cedar that would provide some protection from the wind and snow, and likely serve as his final resting place. In utter exhaustion, he collapsed into the midst of them.

Clumsily, he rolled onto his back and stared upward into a swirling snow globe of bleached whiteness. He had no idea how close he was to Beaver Bay, the lake, or anything that might save him from his now seemingly unavoidable fate. He shuddered as he considered the possibility that he had been wandering in circles for the last hour or two. While the wind seemed to push him forward in a steady direction, at times it switched and swirled in every direction, causing confusion. He thought of Ben Stock and how he had let him down. "I'm sorry Ben" he mumbled, realizing that his face and lips were nearly as numb as his feet and hands.

For several minutes he laid there, his heart pounding so hard that he could feel it in his eardrums. Despite the exertion, his body was quickly cooling, and he shivered as sweat turned to ice. After several minutes, an odd thought struck him: where am I headed? Why I am lying outside in a blinding snowstorm? It took several seconds of intense focus for the mental fog to part. He now recognized that he was facing another potent enemy; hypothermia.

As a physician in northern Minnesota, he was all too familiar with the deadly affects associated with the dramatic cooling of the human body. This cooling, labeled hypothermia from the Greek words for 'under' and 'temperature' was first described in the medical journals in 1890. Andersen had witnessed how quickly sailors would die, if they had the sorry misfortune to land in the frigid waters of Lake Superior. Oddly, Martin now recalled a medical journal article he had read several years back, that explained how many of the victims of the *RMS Titanic* disaster did not drown, but died of hypothermia after just 30 minutes in the icy waters of the north Atlantic.

Confusion and panic so electric that it could cause victims to tear off their clothes as they were freezing to death, was a tragic signal that hypothermia had taken control of their minds. Martin recognized that he was starting to lose his grip on reality as his thoughts wandered back to a short story he had read by a popular outdoor writer named London who chronicled a man's slow passage into death as the result of hypothermia. Martin knew he was on death's doorstep.

Then, amazingly, the snow globe above his head stopped swirling. The bitter wind no longer howled, and the torrents of heavy snow stopped falling. Martin wondered if he were now in a dream; maybe dying, maybe even dead. He felt no pain, just a satisfying calm that he had never experienced. And then from nowhere, it appeared; a vision, an apparition. Slowly emerging from the pure white background a young girl, pretty and blond, wearing a long, flowing olive-colored dress appeared. Inexplicably, she seemed to be skimming across the top of the snow, coming directly toward him.

Instinctively he rubbed his eyes and shook his head trying to clear this mind. Analytically he whispered to himself, "Yes, hypothermia is setting in."

Then as she drew near, a broad smile blessed her face and she waved her hand, seemingly inviting Martin to follow her. Spinning around, she began to slowly drift away. Driven by his will to survive, he summoned the last reservoirs of energy from his spent body and stumbled after her.

She moved without effort, floating over the frozen snow drifts that Martin painfully waded through. Just when he knew that one more step was impossible, the girl stopped and faced him. The sweet young girl smiled and appeared to be pointing at something with her left arm. Straining his eyes to penetrate the impending darkness, Andersen spotted what appeared to be a small cabin. Smoke poured from a rusty metal chimney that poked through the flat roof, a single tiny window was glowing a dim orange.

Andersen now looked back to where the girl had been. She was gone; if indeed she had ever been there. Then, as suddenly as it had stopped, the wind began to howl and the snow began to cascade from the heavens as thickly as before.

Chapter 45

Before the first traces of morning sun began to seep into Sally's room, she was up and dressed. She lit the coal-burning stove to ease the morning chill, and to boil up a pot of coffee. Martin, still groggy, rolled over to watch Sally as she worked. They had fallen asleep, clinging to each other in a tight embrace forced by the size of Sally's small bed, and passion that had filled their night of unbridled love-making. For Martin it was an experience he could not have anticipated, or even describe. For Sally, it was the first time that tenderness or maybe even a feeling of love was part of the sexual act. It took her by complete surprise.

Sally noticed that Martin was now awake, and she smiled affectionately at him. "Doctor, your patients are a waiting, better get yourself movin," she teased. He responded with a fond and pleasing smile.

"They can wait a bit. Come back to bed. What are you so busy doing?"

Instantly, Sally's sweet smile was replaced by a grim expression. "Martin, I'm leavin'…leavin' Duluth."

For a moment, Andersen wondered if he was still asleep, caught up in a strange and disappointing dream. He was, unfortunately, fully awake and Sally's words did not surprise him as much as he might have expected.

Martin fumbled for the right words. While he felt a burning desire for this pretty young girl, how could he, a respected doctor in a respectable hospital have anything more than physical relationship with a 'scarlet woman'? What would the community or his family think? He lay quietly for a moment considering his options. It was obvious that Sally was scared and in a hurry. She pulled up the pine chair next to her bed, and took Martin's hand in hers.

Martin made a meager attempt to convince her to stay. "Don't go Sally. Stay here with me. I'll, I'll protect you…." Whether it would have made a difference or not, Martin's words sounded hollow, bordering on insincere. Sally was not surprised, and in some ways relieved; it would be easier to leave now.

"Martin, we both know this will ne'er work between us. You're a righteous man, a respected man, and I am, well you know," her voice faded to silence. "Besides, I would be fearin' for me life, if I stayed here, so I'm goin' to Minneapolis to start fresh. If you would be agreeable, I'll send you a post from time to time?"

Martin raced through a list of ideas he hoped might stall or prevent this sudden, sad good-bye. But for each option that brought hope, he discovered several reasons why it would not work. Still naked, he self-consciously wrapped the bed sheet around his waist, as he stood and reached for Sally. Without a word, he took her in his arms, holding her tightly in a long embrace, not wanting to let her go. When he finally did, he stepped back, and carefully slid an intricately carved silver band from his ring finger.

"This was my grandfather's," Martin said somberly, cradling the ring reverently in the palm of his hand. "He was a great man, a respected doctor in Sweden. This ring, his ring, carries the Rod of

Asclepius, an ancient Greek symbol of knowledge and healing. He gave it to me, when I came to America. Please take it. May it bring you healing, and protect you from harm."

"Martin, I can't. It is too special to you, and you will be needing it."

Martin stared deeply into Sally's eyes. "I want you to have it. It will remind you of me, until we see each other again." He slid the ring on the index finger of Sally's right hand. Her eyes filled with tears, as she wrapped herself around Martin, squeezing him as tightly as she could. Maybe, maybe someday she would be able to come back, and then...."I got to be going, Martin. The train leaves at half-past eight, and I have no more time."

With that, she picked up her grip and headed out the door. As Martin watched her disappear through the doorway, he wondered if he would ever see her again.

Chapter 46

Willis Chambers' passionate hope that the Venture Club 'issue' would evaporate, was dashed four days later. He had just finished breakfast and walked the fifty feet to his office to find one of his deputies, Isaiah Pike, sitting at the Sheriff's desk. Pike was clearly in a state of elevated animation. New to the police force, he was young, and eager to do real law man work.

"Just got a telephone call from the watch man down at the Torrey Building," the deputy said excitedly. There was a long pause, as the young lawman waited for some sort of authoritative response from the Sheriff. None was immediately forthcoming.

"And...?" Chambers finally replied as he collapsed into a large chair in the corner of his office.

"A jumper," Pike replied authoritatively, projecting the feigned air of confidence from one trying to hide their inexperience.

"Dead?"

"As a doornail!"

Suicides were not uncommon in Duluth, as every so often someone found the need to remove themselves from this life, hoping for something better in the next. However, most chose a pistol or rifle to complete the deed. Jumpers were rare. "Well, go down there and pick up the body, take it to the morgue," Chambers replied coldly. As an afterthought, Chambers asked, "Did the watchman have any idea who it was?"

"Yes, I wrote it down." The deputy flipped through his quickly scribbled notes. "It was a Mr. …..Mr. Anders Johnson. I guess he has business offices on the top floor."

Willis Chambers felt a cold shiver slither down his spine. He knew that Johnson was an influential businessman, and a member of the Duluth Venture Club. He wiped the back of his hand across his forehead, as beads of sweat suddenly began to collect there.

"You sure about that?' he asked nervously.

"Yes sir!"

"Let's go." Chambers gathered himself up from the comfortable chair, while jamming his uniform hat on his head. He stepped with purpose through the doorway with Deputy Pike trailing behind like a frisky pup.

After a few minute's walk along the still sleepy downtown streets, they arrived at the Torrey Building. Once there, they quickly located the watchman, a fellow named Branch, standing patiently next to a thick grey blanket draped over something large and round. As they approached it was impossible to ignore the bright red rivulet of blood springing from beneath the blanket, running 30 or so feet down the sidewalk along 4th Avenue.

Sheriff Chambers nodded toward the watchman. "When did this happen?" Chambers inquired as he gingerly lifted the blanket, and took a quick look at the broken and crumpled body underneath.

Don't really know for sure. Found him here when I come on duty at seven this morning." For emphasis, Branch shot a thick stream of tobacco juice through pursed lips, painting a brownish streak on the red cobblestone street. Shaking his head, he added, "Don't know why someone like Mr. Johnson would do

207

this."

"You talk to anyone upstairs?"

Branch turned his head, and launched another stream of tobacco juice into the street. "No one around earlier. S'pose someone's up there now."

Sheriff Chambers tried to ignore the fact that the sidewalk was covered with shards of window glass, but the eager young deputy was quick to inform his boss about the obvious clue. "Sheriff, don't it seem odd that if the man was going to jump, that he wouldn't open the window first?"

Chambers had to admit that it *was* odd, but was busily trying to construct a circumstance that didn't include the possibility of murder. His gut told him that this death was somehow connected to the events that had taken place at Tettegouche Camp a week ago, and it was a nasty box of snakes he didn't care to open. "Coulda, been an accident," Chambers said firmly as he shoved his hands deep into his uniform jacket pockets.

"An accident?" Deputy Pike was astounded. "How?"

"Fellow may have tripped, fallen up against the window pane, and she gave way." Before he finished the sentence, Chambers felt sheepish for even suggesting it. "Anyway, you get the body over to the morgue, and I will go upstairs and check things out."

Pike was crestfallen as he was eager to investigate the scene of the crime or accident. Disposing of corpses was not his idea of real law man work.

Chambers made his way to the front of the Torrey Building which looked out on Superior Street. Passing through the towering atrium, he stepped into the middle of three elevators located in the spacious lobby. He nodded casually at the elevator operator who was dressed in a neatly pressed, dark blue uniform decorated with shiny gold shoulder epaulets.

"Where to Sheriff?"

"Top floor."

The operator slid the door of the heavy wrought iron cage closed and pushed the control lever as far up as it would go. The elevator rattled and shook as it slowly climbed the dizzying heights to the 12th floor. "I heard about Mr. Johnson," the elevator man commented as they passed the fifth floor. "Such a nice man… always had a pleasant word. You wonder why someone like that…got everything going for him, would end it all."

Chambers shrugged his shoulders. "Anybody else been up here this morning?"

"Well, I come on at seven. Mr. Johnson is always the first one in…such a hard worker. Since I been here, just the regulars. They all been talking about Mr. Johnson." The elevator lurched, clanged and slammed to a stop. The operator yanked opened the cage. "Here you are Sheriff; their offices are to the right."

Chambers nodded and stepped into the dark hallway, heading toward the glass doors that neatly displayed the name **A.J. Johnson and Associates** in fancy gold leaf lettering. Chambers opened the door and entered a brightly lit reception room. A well-dressed young girl sat behind a tidy desk. Her eyes were blood-shot, and it was clear that she was been crying. Chambers quickly snatched the hat from his head.

"Mornin' miss. I'm Sheriff Chambers. I'm here to check on the *incident* that happened here this morning. Can you direct me to Mr. Johnson's office?" The girl dabbed her eyes with a rumpled handkerchief with her left hand while pointing toward the office door with her right. The whole office was as quiet as a tomb.

Slowly opening the door, the Sheriff stepped into Johnson's impeccably neat and spacious office. The dark oak walls were covered with artist drawings of buildings, bridges and piers. The corner office was unusually bright due to the row of five foot windows on each of the two outside walls. The only sound was the wind coming off the lake that whistled through the broken window to the left of his impressive desk.

Chambers, who had a nasty fear of heights, edged cautiously toward the broken window; finally locating a spot where he was as far back from the window as possible while still able to snatch a quick glance to the street below. He saw that his deputy and the watch man had been joined by a growing collection of curious gawkers.

"Good morning Sheriff."

Chambers jumped at the unexpected voice behind him. Instinctively, he spun around, nearly losing his balance. There in the office doorway stood Arlo Peterson.

"Mr. Peterson…..what brings you…..here?"

"Oh, I heard the tragic news about my good friend Mr. Johnson, and I had to come right over." Peterson spoke with an exaggerated tone of empathy and remorse.

"Looks like a suicide, to me," Chambers offered without prompting.

"Yes, I'm afraid it does," replied Peterson, without even looking at the window. "I guess it is puzzling when a successful man like Johnson, well-liked and well-respected in the community is driven to such a tragic end. We just never know what is in a person's mind and soul. Do we?"

210

Chambers did not require much convincing, but was still bothered by the window glass strewn in the street below. "The sidewalk is covered with broken glass. Any clue why someone planning to jump wouldn't open the window first?" Chambers was hoping that Peterson might have a plausible explanation. Arlo did not disappoint.

Without hesitation, Peterson shot back, "those windows are fixed, and there is no way to open them." Chambers stared at Peterson, pausing to consider his statement. Seeing the Sheriff's startled reaction, Peterson quickly added, "Well, that is what I would presume anyway."

Chapter 47

It may have been a whiff of the putrid combination of rancid meat, wood smoke, and kerosene that eventually yanked Martin Andersen from his dreamless, deathlike sleep. As he forced his eyes opened, he had no idea what he would see; his mind now cloaked in a thick mental fog.

As he did, a chocolate brown, heavily lined face hovered above him. "You alive, mister?" the man asked with a bit of a chuckle. His thick black hair, streaked with strands of grey was pulled tightly into braids that hung down over each shoulder. Long strings of colorful beads dangled from the lobes of his ears. His dark, murky eyes reflected a genuine look of concern.

Martin blinked several times, trying to comprehend where he was. As he began to emerge from his stupor, waves of pain radiated from his hands and feet. "Where am I?" Martin whispered hoarsely, trying to decide if he was dreaming, or dead.

"My cabin," the man answered with a faint trace of pride. He smiled a wide grin that revealed a mouthful of discolored and broken teeth. "I am Austin White Feather. You are a lucky man," he continued. "I heard a loud noise last night, and found you outside my door…I thought it was the Ashibishidosh, the spirits of our ancestors coming to take me to the sky."

Andersen's whole body ached as painfully twisted his

head from side to side, surveying his new surroundings. The cabin was not much larger than the servant privies that stood behind the stately mansions on London Road, though not nearly as well built. The walls were a patchwork of assorted pieces of rough sawn lumber. Hewn log rafters supported a rusty tin roof. A small wood stove burned fiercely in the corner, its rusty metal chimney disappearing through the roof. The furnishings, if one could call them that, consisted of a single chair, a ratty and smelly bearskin covered mattress on the floor where the doctor now lay, and a large wooden box.

"How bad are my hands and feet?" Martin asked the Ojibwe cautiously.

"Not good," he replied mournfully, waggling his head slowly. Andersen held his hands in front of his eyes. The skin was a waxy mottled mix of red and purple, and as he slowly clenched his fingers, even sharper waves of pain shot down his wrists.

"Feet the same," reported White Feather regretfully. From around the single, poorly sealed window, a few flakes of snow filtered into the room, floating on a cool breeze until the warmth of the stove returned them to vapor. Sunlight poured in through the small window, letting Martin know that much time had passed.

"How long have I been here?" Andersen inquired, still trying to reconstruct the events that led him to this place.

"Many hours," White Feather replied as he took a small dented, coffee pot from the top of the wood stove. Cautiously, he poured a pale brown liquid into a small tin cup. "Here, drink," he insisted, sticking the steaming cup under Martin's nose. The sickly odor reminded the doctor of embalming fluid.

"What is it?" he asked with a hoarse tinge of disgust. Though his mouth was as dry as a desert wind, he found it hard to sip the nasty potion.

"Cedar root tea," Austin replied as he forced the cup closer to Martin's lips. "It will help you."

As Martin's mind continued to clear, he now recalled the blinding snow, the bitter cold, and the.. the girl; or was *that* a dream? But now, gratefully, he realized that he had survived. He didn't know how, or why. But he owed it to Ben Stock, and Sally to get back to Duluth and bring this savagery to an end.

"How far are we from Beaver Bay?"

"About half a day's walk."

Martin was stunned. After the hardship he had endured, he was certain that he had gotten closer than that. "How far are we from Tettegouche Camp?" Austin gave him a sideways glance, seemingly unsure how to answer the question. "Do you know the camp, log cabins, near three lakes?"

Austin now flashed a jagged toothy grin. "Where Sarge lives?" he said excitedly.

"You know, Ben Stock, eh Sarge?"

"Yes, I know him well; a good man."

Martin felt compelled to tell Austin about the heroic but heartbreaking end to Ben's time on this earth, but decided to withhold the mournful news for now. "I need to get to Beaver Bay. Will you help me?"

The savvy Ojibwe shook his head vigorously. "You must rest and there is much snow."

Still holding the cup under Martin's nose, Austin was finally able to induce him to drink some of the root tea, which, despite its disagreeable smell, tasted pretty good. As he tossed several more pieces of firewood into the small stove, Austin said idly, "You look like a dead man."

214

Martin could well image how badly he must appear, certain he may have the mask of death about him, but even so, he found little humor in the Indian's comment. "I look that bad?" he replied with an obvious hint of sarcasm.

"No, I mean you look like the dead man I found near the three lakes some days ago," Austin stated calmly.

Andersen tried to comprehend what the man was saying. "You found a body near Tettegouche Camp?"

"Yes, I heard the voice, I knew someone had died. His throat was slit, he looked like you."

Blood rushed to Martin's head, and he felt like his eyeballs were about to explode. "What are you saying? What voice?" Though still groggy, Martin was beginning to piece together what Austin was trying to tell him. It was more than his mind could handle.

"The *manidoo ikwezens*, the spirit girl," Austin replied reverently. "She lives in the lake. She sings when death is about to visit."

Martin's mind raced back to when he first approached Tettegouche Camp. "What...what day was that?" Martin stammered, as an overwhelming feeling of dread and understanding crashed into him like a locomotive fired with tar and pine knots.

Austin tugged thoughtfully at one of his braids of hair. "Three days ago."

With a sense of shock and surprising sadness, Martin now realized that if what White Feather was telling him was true, the melodic siren call he heard as he approached Tettegouche Camp that first afternoon, was announcing the death of his twin brother.

Chapter 48

In the fall of 1912, the sprawling Howard Sawmill was dismantled and moved to Canada. The vast, seemingly insatiable mill was the grandest in northern Minnesota. Though it burnt to the ground twice during its twenty year existence, each time it was rebuilt larger and more ravenous. During its operation, it had cut and shipped millions of board feet of white pine lumber each year.

While its departure was viewed as just another business decision by most, it would soon become evident that its exodus was a harbinger that the endless forests of northeastern Minnesota were playing out.

By the spring of 1913, as the last of winter's dreary coat of dirty snow was disappearing from Duluth's streets and sidewalks, John Wentworth was busy relocating his bustling law firm to its plush new offices on the 8th floor of the Torrey Building. With a staff of six attorneys and eight legal assistants, Wentworth and Associates was now the largest law firm in the city.

Wentworth continued to encourage and accept all manner of legal cases, calculating that the more desperate and unsavory the client, the larger the fee. His well-earned reputation for 'pulling a rabbit from his hat', as overmatched prosecuting attorneys would often grumble, filled the bulging coffers of his firm. And while no one could offer proof, scuttlebutt around the

County Courthouse was that JW, as he was now known, had at least two of the three circuit court judges on his payroll.

As driven and hardworking as he was cool and calculating, Wentworth was busy reviewing court documents early one April morning in '13 in his spacious new office when like a ghost, Matts Andersen appeared in the doorway.

Wentworth was expecting him. "Come in Matts" he said pleasantly. "Please, sit down." He casually waved his hand toward an overstuffed leather chair that sat squarely beneath the large airy window that looked out over the lake. The soft pink of the impending sunrise shimmered over the great lake, giving Andersen an almost celestial glow as he nodded compliantly and collapsed into the thickly upholstered chair.

Matts was nervous, unsure why he had been summoned. They had not seen each other since the funeral for Anders Johnson. "I have another job for you," Wentworth said flatly, while he continued to rifle through the bundles of paper on his desk.

Matts' bright blue eyes darkened as he focused a fierce glare on Wentworth. "For God's sakes John, when will this end?"

Slowly, Wentworth rocked back in his chair, now noticing that the sky behind Andersen's head was slowly changing from pink, to deep amber and orange. He replied with a churlish tone.

"Let's not go through this again. I have no time, and I'm in no mood to rehash these hand wringing discussions that come up each time I need you to carry out one of my simple requests. You know what will happen if you let me down."

Easily and quickly defeated, Matts cast his eyes toward the floor as he slumped back in his chair. He was trapped by his own despicable actions, and Wentworth's knowledge of them. He felt as if his neck was poised beneath a guillotine, with Wentworth's hand on the rope. He had few, if any options other than to do what he was instructed. Seeing that Andersen's brief resistance had been broken, JW continued.

"I hadn't figured the court would uphold Prescott's claim to the railroad." He confessed with a tone that grew angrier with each word. Despite months of legal wrangling, financial coaxing, and thinly veiled threats, the courts had come down on the side of Alan Prescott. Wentworth had been outmaneuvered by the prickly Irishman and he was almost as upset by his failure to win as he was by the temporary loss of what he wanted most.

"Prescott is in the way."

Chapter 49

As he lay on the smelly bearskin in White Feather's meager cabin, Martin continued to scrutinize the possibility that his brother was dead, murdered. An eerie silence settled into the cabin that was grew darker by the moment as the sun ducked below the horizon. Gradually, it was replaced by an early rise of a perfectly full moon that lit up the fresh layer of snow, and reflected its soft light into the cabin. Martin continued to sip the cedar root tea as Austin opened the wooden box and retrieved several pieces of dark red jerky.

"Moose meat," he announced, handing a large strip to his guest. "Very good." Martin took the dried meat and began to chew vigorously. Though tough, the smoky meat was tasty, and while it soon caused his jaw to ache, it began to slake his gnawing hunger.

"I must go, Mr. White Feather," Martin said abruptly. I must get back to Beaver Bay, so I can return to Duluth." Despite the pain that continued to radiate from his hands and feet, he was fueled by a frenetically percolating brew of remorse, anger, and vengeance.

Austin looked him over carefully and realized that this man would not be easily dissuaded from what he was determined to do. "I will help you," Austin said patiently, "but not this day. The sun is set. We will go in the morning if you are up to it."

Andersen wanted to argue the point, but realized the Ojibwe was making sense. He went back to work on his slowly disappearing piece moose meat. As he chewed, there was a moment he wondered if he could really trust the Indian who held his very existence in his hand. Though most of the violent conflicts between the white man and the red man were now in the past, there still existed for some, an unrelenting hatred borne out of generations of grievances. In the shadowy room, Martin cautiously eyed the Indian, searching for any clue of what White Feather was capable of doing.

Once Austin had finished eating, he lit the cabin's lone kerosene lamp which hung from a rusty nail pounded into one of the log walls. The flame flickered as it spit black threads of smoke from the short glass chimney. Austin slid his chair next to one of the cabin walls, and rocked back until it was precariously propped up against the wall. As he leaned back, Martin noticed that Austin's face almost disappeared into the background. It seemed like a good time to talk.

"So Austin, how did you end up here?" Martin inquired gently. "Aren't most of your people up on Nett Lake?"

Nett Lake, a large, shallow body of water lent its name to the reservation that had been established in northeastern Minnesota; the result of two ill-fated treaties and one presidential order that, in a lopsided bargain, shrunk the homeland of the Ojibwe tribes from millions of acres down to an area of 100,000.

With a forlorn look, Austin nodded slowly. "Yes, but...I would not be locked up in a white man's jail. I sold my allotment and left." He spoke without a hint of animosity. "The great spirit gave us this land. Only he can take it away."

"You speak excellent English. Did you go to school?"

Austin frowned and rocked forward in his chair. "Yes, I was sent to the Morris Industrial School when I was a boy."

Martin had read about these schools which the white man developed as a means to 'civilize' the red man. Without shame, they were described as institutions designed 'to kill the Indian, to save the man.'

"Any family?"

"No, I had a squaw for several winters; she died giving birth to our son." Anticipating Martin's next question, Austin added quickly, "he died too." He rocked backed until his chair was again leaning up against the wall. Martin stopped chewing and cleared his throat.

"Sarge is dead," he blurted out.

Chapter 50

Alan Prescott sat alone in the spacious bar at the Spalding Hotel, nursing a mug of beer and fiddling with the stem winder of his Patek Philippe pocket watch. It was nearly closing time, and only a few, mostly inebriated patrons, were left in the bar.

After a few minutes, Scottie located a table as far away from them as possible and sat down. Several days before, he had received the very best news he could have hoped for. The circuit judge had reviewed the various claims related to wills and Schmidt's estate, and concluded that the original will, the one leaving him as the sole owner of the D&NMR and associated railroads was binding. Prescott was now where he had hoped to be from the moment he had arrived in Duluth.

Several minutes later, the man he was scheduled to meet walked in the door. Spotting Scottie in the corner, he quickly slid into a chair next to him. "I understand that congratulations are in order" he said as waved over the barkeep who was busy cleaning glasses.

"Yep, they're all mine now," Prescott announced with a salacious look on his face. "It's been a long time in coming."

As the barman approached, the two men went silent. "Whatil it be?" he inquired.

"My friend will have what I'm having," Scottie pronounced. Once the beer arrived, and barkeep departed, the two continued their conversation.

"Scottie, I want you to know, that I am willing to help you in <u>any</u> way I can," the man said with a look of sincerity. He took a deep gulp of his beer that left a bit of foam on his upper lip. Taking a bright linen handkerchief from his inside pocket, he neatly wiped away the foamy traces from his clean-shaven face.

"I appreciate that" Scottie replied causally. "I might have a few things that you can do for me. Let me think about it for a couple of days, and I will get back to you."

Once they had finished their drinks and conversation, they got up to leave. "Let me get this," Scottie offered, as he dropped a couple silver dollars on the bar. As they stepped out into the cool night air, the streets were dark, and quiet. One horse cab was posted nearby, and the man motioned for the cabby to come and pick them up.

"I would just as soon walk home," Scottie announced. But his companion would have none of it.

"No, the ride is on me. I live out east of you. I can drop you off on the way by." The man grabbed Scottie's arm and helped him into the back seat of the carriage. With a snap of the whip, the obedient horse took off with a spritely gait eventually turning on to London Road. Once they had made the turn, the roadway became nearly black, the only light now coming from the battery powered headlamps of the carriage.

After a few minutes, the driver suddenly and severely hauled back on the reins, and the horse came to a clumsy stop. The words 'what are we stopping for' had barely passed Scottie's lips when his companion turned and buried a six inch knife into Prescott's chest. Blood streamed from the wound and dripped from the handle of the knife blade as Scottie desperately gasped for air. The driver now urged the horse forward along the dark empty street.

When the carriage reached Tischer Creek the two men pulled Alan Prescott from the cab, and hurried tossed him into the rapidly flowing creek below. Whether the knife wound, the fall, or the cold creek water ultimately killed Alan Prescott would never be determined as the fast moving waters of the creek delivered Prescott to an unmarked watery grave at the bottom of Lake Superior.

Chapter 51

By 1915, Duluth had again become a noisy beehive of activity as a distant European war created an insatiable demand for iron ore, timber and food staples. A new shipyard was constructed in the harbor that was soon turning out ocean bound freighters; eight a time. Within the year, the Port of Duluth was again among the busiest in the world.

Train cars on the Duluth and Northern Minnesota rail lines ran incessantly, as loggers were ferried further and further north, stopped only by the Canadian border, to fill waiting flatbeds with logs. John Wentworth, who now controlled the railroad, after the unexpected disappearance, and presumed death of Alan Prescott in the spring of '13, pushed man and machine as hard as he could to meet the lucrative demand.

At St. Luke's, Dr. Martin Andersen's life had returned to its normal, if breakneck pace. For weeks and then months he had anxiously awaited a note, or the joyous reappearance of Sally in the flesh. Thoughts of her were never far from his mind; occasionally she appeared in his dreams. In his lonely moments, he cursed himself for his infernal lack of grit in convincing her to stay. He lamented his lack of temerity. And though, he had come to despise his brother in many ways, he felt a tinge of jealousy, certain that if Matts had been in his place, Sally would still be here.

By 1917, as the closure of the Howard Mill had foreshadowed, Comstock-Peterson shuttered the last of it's sawmills in northeastern Minnesota. Like the forest lands to the east, as soon as the inexhaustible bounty of pine and valuable hardwoods had been replaced by a sea of stumps and logging slash, the loggers moved on. Though some of the local logging interests moved to areas around Walker and Bemidji, Minnesota, CP picked up and moved its entire operation to the State of Washington.

Unfortunately, Arlo Peterson, in failing health for several years, was unable to make the move, and was forced to sell his stake in the company he had founded. Two months later, he was found dead in his study by one his maids; an apparent victim of a massive heart attack.

A year later, as the muted orange and yellow colors of autumn began to emerge throughout the City of Duluth and surrounding hills, two great calamities struck the city, testing the mettle and resilience of the region's citizens, and its medical providers.

On October 12th , after a summer of rainless, scorching heat, a long smoldering peat fire near the town of Brookston some 30 miles southwest of Duluth, broke its leash. Propelled by winds reaching 60 miles per hour, the snapping, snarling wildfire emerged from the swamps as a raging inferno headed north, consuming everything in its path. Within eight hours, nine Minnesota towns were incinerated, another dozen badly damaged. During the hellish day, 4000 homes were destroyed, and 453 people were killed; not counting the hundreds of Indians who perished, but were not considered worth counting by the white citizens of the area.

That evening, as a pale rose-colored sun settled into a smoke-fill horizon trainloads of burned and terrified survivors flooded into Duluth and nearby Superior, Wisconsin. At St. Luke's Hospital, Dr. Martin Andersen, now hospital administrator, worked alongside his overwhelmed staff for an unbroken 48 hours tending to the injured, comforting the dying. The hallways of the hospital were filled with cots as hospital staff labored frantically to provide whatever care they could manage.

Just two weeks earlier, the Minnesota's State Board of Health confirmed the State's first cases of what was referred to as the Spanish Flu. The deadly influenza which first appeared in U.S. Army camps along the east coast had charged across the United States like a stampeding buffalo herd.

Dr. Andersen would identify the first cases of Spanish Flu in Duluth less than a week after the horrific wildfire had burned itself out. Within days, hundreds of residents were afflicted with the disease, which for reasons unknown, was particularly deadly to young adults. St. Luke's was again filled to overflowing with sick and dying patients.

Fortunately, scraps of better news came the following month. On November 11th, an armistice was declared among the warring nations, bringing to an end the unspeakable horror that had become known as the Great War. A week later, a train from St. Paul would deliver six doctors from Chicago who would shore up the area's battle with the sick and injured. And then, as November turned into December, just as quickly as it had appeared, the Spanish Flu outbreak began to subside.

With the passing of years, Martin Andersen began to notice the first hints of grey appearing in his goatee, as wrinkles began to gather around his eyes. He was no longer the county coroner, a job he left when he became St. Luke's hospital administrator. However, as administrator it was his duty to review and sign off on all autopsies conducted in the hospital's morgue. As was his nature, he carefully reviewed the procedures and findings of every autopsy summarized in the seemingly endless pile of handwritten reports.

One particular report described how a set of skeletal remains had been found in a narrow, nearly invisible crevice below the London Road Bridge that spanned the Lester River. Workers conducting maintenance on the bridge stumbled across the body, which was in an advanced stage of decomposition.

The condition of the body, more accurately described as a pile of bones, made identification all but impossible. The only clues the coroner could provide with certainty was that it was a woman, probably in her late twenties or early thirties. The corpse displayed numerous broken ribs, and a twice-fractured skull. Small tufts of red hair were found with the corpse, and scraps of what appeared to be a green dress.

As Dr. Andersen read the report, he thought how regrettably common it was for desperate young women to seek survival or refuge in the Tenderloin District, only to end up dead. Even though prostitution was now illegal in the city, too many women were still forced to trade their bodies for their very existence. And yet, for some, even that precious trade proved insufficient.

As he read on, the last line of report stated that the only personal effect found with the body was a small, but intricately carved silver ring, which the coroner reported, with great surprise, carried the Rod of Asclepius. Martin stopped, and then violently slammed his fist on his desk, as he began to cry uncontrollably.

"Sally" he wailed. "Oh, Sally."

Chapter 52

"Sarge is dead?" A look of sadness and disbelief covered White Feather's face, and caused his body to snap forward. The chair thumped as it landed back on all four legs. "How do you know?"

"I was there. He saved my life."

Now as if a dam had suddenly burst, Martin began to pour out the story of his family life, the interlocking events that included the deaths of the Venture Club members, Sally, and now, most likely his brother. When he finished, he felt a palpable sense of relief. It was only then that he realized that he had been caring these bricks like an overloaded donkey, quiet and uncomplaining, while slowly being crushed by the weight.

Austin remained silent listening, nodding, chewing, and puzzling. Now he had a question. "Why are you in such a hurry to get back to Duluth?"

"I am going to kill the one responsible," Andersen replied with a surprisingly casual tone.

Austin gave him a sidewise look. "Vengeance?"

"Yes. Don't you think I deserve the right to deliver some retribution?"

"Will that bring your brother, or Sarge, or the girl back to life?"

"Of course not," Martin fired back sarcastically, surprised that the Indian was being so reasonable, so humane. Like many of his race, Martin grew up believing that most Indians possessed an innate layer of savagery in their soul that placed human life on a par with a deer or a bear; there for the taking.

"Someone must pay," Martin said without hesitation.

Chapter 53

The winter of '22-3, was the coldest anyone in Duluth could recall. Not only was the harbor frozen solid, it was reported that the entire body of Lake Superior was frozen tight, with several ships trapped in the thick ice, miles from shore, safety, and salvation. Some days, the temperatures never got above zero, with overnight temperatures dropping to 20 to 30 below. Accustomed to winter's bitter bite, the hearty residents of Duluth, for the most part went about their daily duties as always.

After finding the body of Sally Keefe, Martin Andersen had emerged a changed man. He was certain that her death was no accident, nor the work of an unbalanced or unsatisfied 'john'. Her death was somehow tangled up with the growing number of Venture Club member deaths; he was sure of that. This time he would not, could not, let this go without a fight.

On a cold, snowy March morning in 1923 Doctor Andersen paid a visit to the County Sheriff. Though his benefactor, Arlo Peterson was no longer around, Willis Chambers had been able to cling to his post of county sheriff.

"Morning Willis," Martin announced as entered the office, stamping snow from his boots onto the badly stained wood floor. Taken by surprise, Chambers looked up with from his paperwork with a furrowed brow and an odd smile.

"Doc…..my, what brings ya out on such a cold morning?"

The office was toasty warm, and without a word Martin removed his hat, muffler, and knee length coat, draping them on the coat tree that stood near the door. As the Sheriff watched, Martin took the chair in front of the desk. "Sheriff, we need to talk."

It had been years since the two had discussed the mysterious deaths of Thomas Schmidt, Anders Johnson, or the disappearance of Alan Prescott, who was never found; dead or alive. As in the other cases, no suspect had been charged. But that was not what brought Andersen to the office today.

"A woman has been killed, and I want you to open an investigation."

"I got no report of a woman being killed," Willis responded as he leaned forward in his chair.

"Her body was discovered down by the Lester River Bridge and brought to the morgue. She's been dead for some time."

"How long you figure?"

"I'm guessing ten years."

The answer so astonished Chambers that he actually snorted like an agitated boar pig. What kind of joke is this, he thought to himself. "No, seriously, Doc. How long?"

"I am pretty sure about ten years." He glared at the Sheriff who quickly realized that Andersen was deathly serious. Chambers ran his fingers through his thick black hair, buying time to form a reasonable answer to the doctor's outlandish request.

"Doc, you know as well as I do that when someone's been dead that long, there ain't no hope of finding the killer. Where would a person even start?"

"I'm pretty sure this death is tied to deaths of the Venture Club members. I think we start by interviewing those who are left."

Chambers was at a loss. "I don't even remember who they are," the Sheriff pleaded.

Andersen started slowly. "Willis, listen. From what I know, at least five people have been murdered, for reasons that neither you nor I can even guess, much less know. I beg of you, we need to figure out who has done these terrible things, and bring them to justice."

Chambers stared down at his desk, suddenly ashamed. He knew, despite his efforts to hide behind the easy way out, the doctor was right. In fact, it had been eating at him for years. It was pretty clear that the deaths of the Venture Club members were not accidents, but well planned murders. And that the murderer or murderers expected that they would never be discovered.

"You're right Doc. Tell me what you want me to do?"

Chapter 54

While Martin slept fitfully on the course, noxious bearskin, the Indian slept soundly sitting in the chair propped up against the rickety wall. Once or twice during the night when Martin stirred to semi-consciousness, he marveled at Austin, poised precariously on two shaky chair legs, fixed in a trance, his head tilted back against the log wall, breathing softly. He wondered what the man was dreaming, if indeed he dreamed at all.

Finally, as the first dim rays of sunlight crept into the solitary window, Austin began to stir. The woodstove had burned to ashes during the night, and the cabin was freezing. Picking up several handfuls of tinder, he tossed them into the stove. Soon, the slumbering ashes sprung to life. As flames began to lick the sides of the open door, Austin tossed in four larger pieces of firewood and slammed the door closed. A minute later, he was up and out the door. When he reappeared he was wearing a broad smile, and toting a large piece of meat in each hand.

"I shot a deer two days ago, and got it hanging on the meat pole," Austin explained noticing Martin's puzzled look. With the return of colder weather, fresh, if mostly frozen meat was now readily available.

Austin scraped the remains of some previous meal from the bottom of a badly blackened cast iron fry pan onto the floor as Martin cautiously examined his hands and feet. To his relief, though ugly and painful blisters covered his fingers and toes, there was no sign of blackened flesh. Black meant dead tissue, which usually required amputation of toes, fingers, or even hands and feet. While the pain was still intense, his feeling of relief was palpable.

Soon the crackling sound and pleasant aroma of frying venison mixed with onions began to mask, at least for a while, the nose curdling odors that had filled the room. Seeing the doctor examining his hands and feet, Austin provided his own diagnosis.

"I seen worse."

Martin nodded as he struggled to sit up on the bearskin, and prop his back against the cold wall. "I am ready to head to Beaver Bay, Austin. Will you help me?"

White Feather nodded, apparently more concerned with his cooking then a long trek though mountains of fresh snow. Without looking up, he announced "I've got an extra pair of snowshoes. Have you 'shoed before?" Again, Martin was faced with a new experience. But a growing confidence in his abilities to meet new challenges was starting to reshape the man he had been for almost 40 years.

"I'll learn, don't worry about me."

Austin smiled, as his head bobbed up and down like that of a child's wooden toy. For a moment, Martin just stared. 'He must have so many stories to tell' Martin thought to himself.

After their warm, gut-filling breakfast had disappeared, they began to prepare for the trip to the lake. Austin handed Martin a thick pair of deer hide boots that laced to the knee, and a sturdy pair of leather mittens that felt warm and soft to his skin. It wasn't until they were headed out the door that Andersen realized that the Ojibwe had given him his only boots and mittens. "I can't take these, what will you wear?" Martin was insistent.

But Austin would have none of it. "No need to worry about me," he replied calmly, "I have my moccasins and deep pockets in my jacket."

After he had finished lacing up his boots, Martin wobbled to his feet. Searing pain shot from the soles of his feet nearly to his knees. For a moment he almost buckled, but he was not to be stopped. As he cautiously headed toward the door, Austin couldn't help but laugh. "You walk like a drunken bear."

As they stepped out of the cabin, the brilliant morning sun poured through the treetops reflecting across the pure white landscape. The combination was blinding. Even after several minutes, Martin found it difficult to pry open his eyes far enough to even see where they were going.

Leaning up against the side of the cabin were two pair of bent wood snowshoes. Martin was certain that Austin had crafted these fine 'shoes' as they were made in the traditional Objibwe style. As he picked one up, he was suddenly reminded that his father would sell these snowshoes at his dry goods store. "Handmade Ojibwe snowshoes, best you can buy" his father would tell prospective customers as they eyeballed the intricate lacing and bindings.

After a little tugging and pulling, and a handful of instructions from Austin, the two men set out. Austin went first, vigorously attacking the exhausting task of breaking trail through knee deep snow and tangled underbrush. Though clearly not a young man, Austin easily muscled through the deep snow, his legs churning like the pistons of a new steam engine with a hot fire and a full load of water. Martin followed hesitantly, trying to develop a rhythm of walking on the long, cumbersome snowshoes.

Despite the advantage of following in a packed trail, Andersen plunged nose first several times as the tip of his snowshoe caught on snow or brush. He quickly discovered that getting to one's feet after such a fall was harder than staying upright. But after a while, he started to find a sustainable stride that allowed him to keep pace with White Feather.

As they walked, Austin kept up a steady patter; pointing out interesting natural features, and the spot where Austin had shot his first bear with a bow and arrow "the old boar chased me up a birch sapling....would have still been waiting for me to come down, if he hadn't bled to death first." The Indian cackled like a blue jay, sending a warm echo through the pristine, snowy wilderness.

The air was still and much less bitter than when Martin had stumbled onto Austin's cabin. And for the first time since he ventured from Beaver Bay, Martin began to understand and appreciate the beauty and tranquility of the wilderness. His eyes were now open, literally and figuratively. As they continued, Austin would point out fresh deer or wolf tracks. Occasionally, a grouse that had sought shelter in the deep snow drifts would explode from its cover, startling Andersen.

Gratefully, Austin stopped frequently, allowing Andersen a chance to catch his breath. After several hours, Martin noticed that the thick forest seemed to open up, and within a few hundred more yards Austin stopped. As Martin approached, he saw that the land began to fall away, and in the distance, the cold, crystalline waters of Lake Superior shimmered for as far as the eye could see. A wave of relief washed over Andersen as he realized that he had escaped death, at least for now. As he came up behind the Indian, Austin turned and faced him. He had a strained look on his weathered face.

"Doctor, I am wondering. What you have decided. Are you going to kill the man who has brought you such anguish and pain?"

Andersen nodded quickly and firmly. "It is that very thought that has kept me alive, kept me going. I needed to survive if for no other reason than to seek justice for the memories of the people who have died for reasons I don't understand."

Though the midday sun hung low in the southern sky, it shone brightly. As Austin stood at the crown of the long slope leading down to the lake, the sun appeared to be a glowing crown atop his head. Martin shaded his eyes with his left hand, as he waited for Austin to respond.

"Mr. Andersen, over the years I have seen plenty of death. Some brought on by your people, some by members of my own tribe. I can't remember one death that accomplished anything other than quenching the dark spirit that is buried in the soul of many men. You have every right to be angry and expect justice for this man, but are you the one that your God has selected to carry out that justice?" With that, Austin turned and headed down the long slope that led to Beaver Bay.

For a moment, Martin stood frozen, contemplating the weighty words that now hung in the air like a thick cloud of mosquitoes. More confused than ever, he followed the Indian toward Beaver Bay.

Chapter 55

For several days, John Wentworth had been eagerly awaiting news related to the business that needed doing at Tettegouche Camp. A week earlier, he had hailed Matts and laid out his new request.

"It seems that brother of yours is trying to cause trouble, again," Wentworth reported. "I heard from some of my sources that Sheriff Chambers is going to open an investigation into the deaths of the Venture Club members, and some Irish whore, who turned up dead." Wentworth shook his head in disbelief. "And now with Arlo Peterson dead, the Sheriff appears less likely to ignore the pleas of your do-gooder brother."

"Those things are long past," Matts reminded him. "Nobody even remembers Schmidt or Johnson, and Prescott has no more friends now, then he did when he was alive."

"I know that," Wentworth snapped; always aggravated when someone insisted on telling him something he already knew. "But I heard that your brother is going to the newspapers with this story, hoping to force the mayor, or the county board, to do something."

Almost sure that he already knew the answer, Andersen asked cautiously, "so what do you want me to do about it?"

"He needs to disappear!"

"What does that mean?" Matts replied with a shrill, protesting tone. He was just beginning to understand the demonic measures the lawyer was willing to take to protect himself and all he had labored so aggressively to accumulate.

Idly staring out of his office window, Wentworth slowly drummed his fingers on the top of his desk; apparently hoping, expecting that his agile mind would be able to formulate a clean, permanent solution to this latest logjam. "We need him to disappear, literally. Someplace where there will be no corpse, nothing to investigate, just disappear." Wentworth waved his hand like a burlesque house magician attempting to conjure up a rabbit from inside a large beaver skin hat.

"But how can you do that?" Matts was becoming more agitated, and could feel he was reaching a point that he could not cross. Though he had no love for his brother, this was a riverbank too far.

Thinking out loud, JW began laying out his plan. "We need to get your brother to meet you somewhere, so far from town that no one will ever discover what happened; somewhere in the wilderness.

"I won't do it, John."

"Oh, you'll do it alright. You have no choice. And to make sure you follow through, I'll have a couple of my.... associates go with you just to make sure the work gets done."

Chapter 56

After thanking Austin for his friendship and generosity, and giving him a warm, if awkward hug, Dr. Martin Andersen crawled into the motorcar headed toward Knife River. Due to the warming effects of the lake, little snow had accumulated along the cratered road that followed the north shore of the lake. It was almost as if he had left one world and slowly entered another.

Every muscle and sinew ached, his body caked in total exhaustion. His hands and feet burned, and his leg muscles began to tighten within just a few miles. Despite the bone-jarring ride, Martin was soon sound asleep. Three hour later, after catching the last run of the Lake Front line back to Duluth, Andersen finally arrived back at the Duluth station. Though it had been only six days, it seemed like a year had passed since he had had departed. The snow covered streets looked dirty, the buildings dark and gloomy.

As he slowly and painfully trudged the three blocks from the station to his house, he reflected on the people and events of the last few days. It was dream, or more accurately a nightmare he could never forget, nor probably ever escape. Finally arriving home, he headed straight to the water closet. Staring into the mirror above the sink in his tiny washroom, he saw a man he could bearly recognize. A thick layer of stubble now covered his cheeks and neck. His skin was raw and red, a few frostbitten boils still present on his cheeks and ears. His eyes were sunken and glazed. The hair on his head was dirty, greasy, and looked as if he had been riding the cars with his head out the window.

"My God," Martin whispered to man in the mirror, who now shook his head in stolid disbelief. "Maybe Dr. Andersen did die at Tettegouche Camp after all."

With that he turned on the water, freshened his shaving cup, and began to apply a thick layer of lather. Firmly grabbing his straight blade razor, he carefully removed every bit of facial hair from his face. Before finally collapsing into bed, he made one phone call.

Chapter 57

As was his routine, John Wentworth arrived at his office well before first light. Work was his life, winning was his reward. When he wasn't working, he was thinking about it.

Entering the reception area, he absently clicked on the overhead light. After collecting a stack of memos and messages from his in-box, he headed into his office. As he stepped through the doorway, he instinctively reached for the push-button light switch while thumbing through the papers in his hand. With eyes still focused on his papers, he slide behind his desk and sat down. It was not until that very moment he realized he was not alone.

"Jesus Christ Matts! You scared the hell out of me!" Wentworth cursed, his voice anxious and strained. It took him only a few seconds to recognize that something in his plan to end the drama surrounding Tettegouche Camp had somehow gone wrong; terribly wrong. He deftly tried to make the best of this situation.

"So good to see you made it back," Wentworth crowed with the energetic sincerity of a snake oil salesman. "I was worried about you, especially when the blizzard hit a few days ago."

"Your henchmen are dead." Andersen spoke so softly that Wentworth could barely hear him.

"What?" Wentworth replied; hearing but not believing.

"I killed them."

It was only then, that JW noticed the envelope lying in Andersen's lap. "Those men I sent with you were under my strict orders to help you. They must have decided to take out on their own." His voice grew more strained and scratchy.

"Really?" Andersen replied with an obvious tone of incredulity. "And that's why you gave them this note?" Andersen flashed the rumpled note he had taken from the dead man's body. Wentworth began to realize that circumstances were spinning out of his control, and decided to take a more forceful approach.

"Sure, I paid them, but they were obviously out for their own gain. Anyway, the job is done, right?"

"Oh, it's done, alright, but now you owe me answers." Andersen took a deep breath.

"Why did you kill that German fellow, Schmidt?"

Wentworth was taken aback by Andersen's directness and attitude, but decided to go along. "I didn't kill him," he relied mildly.

"Who did?" Andersen shot back.

"Prescott."

"You're a liar!"

"No, it's true."

"Then how do you explain these?" Andersen tossed the thick envelope onto Wentworth's desk.

Wentworth opened it and extracted the sheaf of papers. It took only a minute to realize what he had. "Where did you get these?" Wentworth said with an accusatory tone

"From the Camp." Andersen paused and cleared his throat. "It looks to me that you had some sort of arrangement with Schmidt."

245

Wentworth's quick mind began to dissect the situation. He decided that it was time to end this discussion. "I'm done talking. I think it is time for you to go. Leave now before I call the Sheriff."

"That would be fine. Let's call him," Andersen shot back. "I will be glad to explain to him everything I know."

JW rocked back in his chair, and unexpectedly emitted a hearty laugh that came from deep within his belly. Andersen was bewildered by the lawyer's reaction.

"We both know that if the Sheriff comes, I will just have to provide him some information about your little... preoccupation.... your fondness for....the young boys, a fondness that sometimes ended up with those boys disappearing." A smug, self-confident smile erupted on his face.

Andersen's face went ashen, his throat tightened, and his head began to spin. There it was; the noose that his brother had so conveniently provided the contemptible lawyer. A noose Wentworth employed so barbarically to strangle Matts Andersen in order to further the lawyer's plans.

Martin now stood up and slowly withdrew the .45 caliber pistol from his pocket. With an eerie calm he slowly leveled it directly at Wentworth's head. As he did, he slid closer so the barrel of the pistol now hovered directly in the face of the lawyer. Wentworth's eyes grew as wide as saucers and his hands gripped the edge of his desk so tightly, is looked as if he was about to peel off the thick wooden top.

"Matts, what the hell do you think you're doing?"

"Matts is dead," Martin replied as he reached up and pulled the slide of the pistol back. The weapon was now cocked.

For a few seconds, Wentworth was speechless. He had noticed that this man's voice was a bit deeper than Matts; when suddenly and shockingly he realized that he was talking to Matts' twin brother.

"Martin?" Wentworth replied weakly.

"Yes, that's right. So you blackmailed my brother to kill me?" The pistol was just feet from Wentworth's face as Martin clicked off the safety. Wentworth began to tremble uncontrollably in his chair, certain that the good doctor was fully prepared to pull the trigger.

Attempting to employ his most effective skill, his ability to talk his way out of most situations, the lawyer tried to reason with Martin. "You need to believe me. I did not instruct those men to kill your brother. He must have decided that he was not going along with the plan, and they ended up *having* to kill him."

That comment brought Martin more confusion then clarity. Was it possible, that in the end, Matts tried to save his brother, and died in the attempt? It was a muddle that inflicted heart wrenching pain and a moment's hesitation. But Martin was unwavering in his mission to unravel as much of the mystery surrounding Tettegouche Camp as he could. He owed it to himself, to Sally, to Ben.

"Who killed those other men, Prescott and that Anders Johnson?"

"Your brother, and that's the truth," Wentworth said assertively.

"Because if he didn't you would reveal his secret to the Sheriff?" Andersen added.

Wentworth said nothing. He knew that the more he divulged the less likely his chance to wriggle out of this situation. From a legal perspective, it was his word against Andersen's. There was little evidence, outside the letters and note to tie him these crimes. He was savvy enough to know this was a shaky case, if one were to be brought against him at all, especially since two of the three of the judges in the county were on his payroll.

Suddenly, in a vicious backhand motion, Andersen swung the barrel of the pistol across Wentworth's face knocking him onto the floor, while inflicting a deep, bloody gash to his cheek. Unexpectedly, as the lawyer lay on the floor dazed and whimpering, Andersen felt a wave of regret; 'What kind of man have I become?' he thought. His conversation with Austin White Feather came flooding back, and he wondered, 'what am I capable of doing'?

Now as he stood over Wentworth with the pistol trained on his head, Andersen continued his quest to understand all that happened.

"Why did Prescott kill Schmidt?"

"He found out that Schmidt was trying to take over his share of the railroad."

"You found that out too, right? You were in cahoots!"

"Yes," Wentworth replied meekly, holding his now bloody hand to his bloody cheek.

"What about the girl, Sally Keefe, who killed her and why?"

Andersen took a couple steps back as Wentworth, still holding his bloody cheek with his bloody hand, struggled to sit up on floor, resting his back against the side of his desk. "I don't know what you're talking about?"

"The red haired Irish girl….one of your 'mistresses.'"

Wentworth knew, but he was not about to let on. "No really, I don't recall any girl."

With surprising callousness, Andersen viciously kicked JW in the meaty part of his thigh, momentarily causing his leg to go numb. Wentworth bellowed in pain.

"Oh God," Wentworth moaned. "Ok, ok, I had your brother take care of her, too. She knew something about Schmidt's murder, and I couldn't take any chances.

Andersen had heard more than he could handle. Shocked, angry, deflated, he collapsed into the chair where he had been sitting when JW had first arrived. His mind was swirling like a Lake Superior waterspout and for a moment he regretted that he had uncovered the grisly truth.

As Wentworth sat on the floor, though still in severe pain, he realized that part of his body was now partially shielded from Martin's sight. Slowly he reached his left arm around to the front of his desk, and silently opened the bottom drawer; all the while staring at Andersen, who had lowered his pistol, and now wore a glazed, almost catatonic look.

Careful not to reveal any movement, Wentworth felt around in the bottom drawer until he located his chrome-plated Colt Peacemaker, which had been lying in his desk drawer for the last few years; a bit of insurance Wentworth had told himself, in case the attorney was ever confronted by a disappointed client, or an unrepentant criminal.

As Martin sat quietly in the chair, with the pistol in his lap, he tried to decide what to do. With every painful step he had taken during the snowstorm, he had been fortified by the desire to find and kill the man who had wrought such savagery on so many. Now Satan's henchman was in front of him. He owed it to Ben Stock, to Sally, and maybe, just maybe to his twin brother to administer justice. But he was stymied by the words of Austin White Feather suggesting that the fate of this malevolent miscreant, sitting pitifully on the floor in front of him, was in the hands of a higher power. It was not his place to mete out justice.

Suddenly, a brief flash of reflected light emanating from something Wentworth was holding in his left hand, stirred Martin from his thoughts. It was in that moment that Andersen realized that JW was holding an enormous revolver in his left hand. Before he could react, the gun exploded with an ear-shattering blast, followed by a sharp burning pain in Martin's right shoulder. Helplessly, he watched as his own pistol slipped from his hand, and fell to the floor.

Martin now stared into the eyes of the attorney, and recognized the calm, resolute look of a cold-blooded killer. Sensing that he had once again dug himself out of a tight spot, Wentworth slowly and confidently cocked the hammer of his heavy revolver, ready to bring this sordid nightmare to an end, once and for all. As an evil, blood-smeared smile broke across his face, Wentworth uttered a diabolical epitaph: "You lose."

Then strangely, inexplicably, the door of the office's coat closet swung open, revealing the imposing figure of Sheriff Willis Chambers standing in the shadows, a pistol in his right hand.

"Drop the gun, Wentworth. This is done!" Chambers' booming voice filled the room.

Now for one of the few times in his life, Wentworth failed to react in the unruffled, calculating manner that had brought him so much success. If he had taken a moment to assess his situation, it is likely that he could have constructed an elegant legal path to his escape. If he had taken just a moment or two, he might have been able to plot out a scenario of self-defense, and hearsay evidence. But unfortunately for him, he didn't.

Acting from instinct and propelled with adrenaline, he swung the pistol toward Chambers. But he was too slow. Before he was able to pull the trigger, Chambers buried a slug in Wentworth's chest. A moment later, he was dead.

Chapter 58

It was a warm, mostly sunny morning as Dr. Martin Andersen trudged slowly up the long hill to the highest spot in Forest Hills Cemetery; a spot that peered down upon the local luminaries, scoundrels and pioneers who now lay at rest in this peaceful overlook. His right arm was still cradled in a canvas sling as he made the somber, solitary walk. In his left hand, he caressed a beautiful bunch of bright red roses.

As he reached the plain marble gravestone that marked the final resting place of Sally Keefe he turned to gaze out from this lofty promontory toward the long, narrow city of Duluth that formed a dull, if dramatic border to the northwestern edge of Lake Superior. A slight breeze blowing from north, made the air fresh and savory.

He realized that over the years, he, like the city that lay below, had changed significantly. For the better, he was not sure, but change, absolutely. He decided it was time for him to leave this place; there was nothing here for him now. A single tear trickled down his cheek, as he carefully laid the roses on top of Sally's grave marker.

He thought about his brother; his human remains likely scavenged by wolves or bear. Did he deserve the fate that found him? Was he indeed the monster that Wentworth claimed? Whoever Matts truly was, Martin still felt a deep sense of guilt for the way that Martin had thought about and treated his twin. It was a shame that would stay with him for the rest of his life.

A hundred miles away, in the deep forests of the Arrowhead, for the first time in many years, a peaceful calm settled in over the tannic stained waters of Tettegouche Lake.

Acknowledgements

It is said, with good reason, that no one writes a book by themselves; in my case that is doubly true.

In order to paint an accurate, historical backdrop for this fictional story, I took great advantage of the St. Louis County Historical Society collections which provided robust and easily accessible tools. My thanks also go to the Zenith City Press which provided great detail and substantial historical background as well.

Sincere thanks go to my dedicated, capable, and reliable reviewers, who provided honest and invaluable feedback to the numerous drafts that I sent them: Jay Scoggin, a most literate and insightful Renaissance man, and Ray Hitchcock, who despite a fierce battle with ALS, continuously provided valuable feedback. My one great regret that I was unable to publish this manuscript before Ray passed away.

Thanks also go to Adele Smith and Linda Escher who provided the cover graphic. If that image doesn't encourage you to crack open the book, I don't know what will.

Disclaimer

In my attempt to provide a historically accurate backdrop to this novel, I have done extensive research related to the people and places that existed in the Arrowhead during the timeframe of this story.

However, all the characters that drive the plot of this novel are fictional. Two real persons (Leonidas Merritt and Madame Gains) make brief appearances as historical sidebars. Any resemblance to events and characters chronicled in this story, to actual people and activities is purely coincidental.

In particular, the Tettegouche Club, which constructed the Camp, was as far as I can ascertain, a group of well-intentioned conservationists, and not the unsavory gang of antagonists and protagonists portrayed in this story.

Made in the USA
Monee, IL
13 February 2022

90427026R00152